CW01085716

A NOTE ON T

David Edward was born in South East London. He now lives in East London and divides his time between London and Florida. *London Tales* is his first published work of fiction.

London Tales

David Edward

GADFLY

These stories are entirely a work of fiction. The names, characters and incidents portrayed are the work of the author's imagination. Any resemblance to actual persons, living or dead, localities and events is coincidental

First published by Gadfly Entertainment 2008

www.gadfly-ent.com

This paperback edition published 2008

Copyright © 2008 David Edward

All rights reserved

The moral right of the author has been asserted

A CIP catalogue record for this book is available from the British Library

ISBN 978-0-9559290-0-7

Typeset by Palimpsest Book Production Limited, Grangemouth, Stirlingshire

Printed in Great Britain by CPI Antony Rowe, Chippenham, Wiltshire

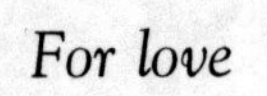

For love

CONTENTS

London Tales

MONSTER

I won't risk another session with these guys, so I decide to go along with what they want. And I'm guessing they want to see if the story I gave them holds against the visuals the technician compiled while they were knocking me around the control room.

Now they've sat me on a wooden chair with my bare back to them and with my face a metre away from a yellowing flip chart. A mug of coffee is shoved into my left hand. I sense the composition of the room has changed. Out has gone the technician and I feel another pair of eyes on me – someone with a greater authority than those who dragged me from the top of the escalator and into this control room. The windows have now been blacked out, even though I suspect the station has already been closed to the public. My whole body, but especially my wrist, aches. But I'm strangely detached from my pain. I can hear the beeps and whirr of audiovisual equipment behind me. I take a sip of the coffee. It's already cold. And then I suspect that what I've been given is the quickly collected remains of what they'd been drinking ten minutes before, when they were gazing at the monitors here in the control room of Piccadilly Circus tube station.

As soon as I sense I have their full attention, and for the benefit of the newcomer, I start again.

It was 11.15 a.m. when I arrived here at the station. I know that, because even in my mad rage a part of me was calm enough to set my bags down for a second and to glance at my watch as I rode the downward escalator to the Heathrow train. At a push, I figured I could still make it to the terminal before the check-in deadline.

I won't argue if, later, your lip-readers claim I was cursing as I came down that escalator. As I said, I was in a raging mood. Only minutes earlier, on the street above, I'd had an incident with Brenda. Voices had been raised and there may even have been the odd shove before I grabbed my two cases from the back seat of the taxi and headed for the tube entrance. I didn't think we had the time to sit arguing with each other in a cab in the middle of the gridlocked traffic. Action was required. In time, I hoped she would see sense and follow my lead. I would have run down, but my path was blocked by a line of tourists. It had been years since I'd used the tube network. I couldn't recall whether this was normal traffic volume for a Saturday. On the spot marked out for buskers, near the foot of the escalator, a woman in a floral summer dress stoically strummed an acoustic guitar as po-faced iPod- and MP3-listening commuters trundled by her. After what I'd just gone through with Brenda, her chirpy song was a mockery of the mood I was in. By the time I got to the mouth of the platform entrance, the sound of her voice was receding and my arms ached under the weight of the bags. They happened to be the only two unwheeled luggage holders we'd taken.

One thing that did come back to me right away – even before I'd dumped the bags at my feet – was that mixture of oil, heavy machinery and bodily exhalations that give the London tube its inimitable scent. The platform was crammed. I glanced up at the destination board, and the timings till the next Heathrow-bound train gave me a sinking feeling. I kept my jacket on, and patted myself down, to reassure myself that my passport was still in my inside pocket. I looked around again. One year in the English countryside was all it had taken for me to lose my ease with the teeming range of human diversity on these tube platforms.

Furthermore, I was still shaken by what had happened up there with Brenda. Added to the anger and frustration was a sense of shame. It was the closest I've ever come to being physically aggressive with her. But it had been a spontaneous thing. No more than the type of dispute two strong-minded people will always have.

A hissing sound jolted me out of my reflection, and I turned and instantly recognised the guy holding the small, plastic Coke bottle. He took a sip, then returned the bottle to a khaki-coloured pouch. The memories of him that now came to me were neither negative nor positive. We'd attended the same secondary school, where he was in the year above mine. He was part of a group my older brother used to run with. He'd taken a year out so we'd ended up in the same year at university, him doing Biochemistry and me doing Physics. We'd also ended up on the same campus and shared some mutual friends back there. He was a skinny little guy then, someone always on the edge of things rather than directing them.

Some four years on, he looked a much-improved physical specimen. He wore trainers, tracksuit bottoms and a sleeveless Puffa jacket. Apart from the khaki pouch, he also carried an Adidas sports bag. He gave the impression that he was on his way to or from the gym.

I leaned forward. "Hey!"

He was about the only person within my sight range not wearing headphones attached to a mobile phone or iPod. He turned, and after a moment, a look of recognition came over his face. He did not smile but his expression wasn't unfriendly. There was a moment's indecision about who should come to whom. I pointed to the heavy luggage between my feet and he slowly picked up his sports bag and ambled over. He wore a calm, serene expression. A close, clean shave gave his face an implausibly youthful appearance.

"Bloody hell," he said. "If it's not old Jonah."

"How're you doing?" I smiled. "Looking well, man."

"Thank you."

"And very serene. Under the circumstances."

He glanced at the destination board. "You have to be. You have to be calm."

"Where are you going?" I asked him. I wanted to be friendly, but I also wanted to pace myself. I wanted to be clear early on how long I would have to spend chitchatting with him.

He hesitated for a brief moment. "I'm off to meet friends."

"But whereabouts?" I pressed. "I guess it's got to be

West London," I smiled. "Because you're taking this train, right?"

He smiled lazily. "Well, I've got to go westward to get there."

"Ever see anyone from school?" I asked him. "Or uni?"

"No, not at all," he responded quickly. "Do you?"

"Not so much from school. But we've got a graduate reunion thing going once a year. And I'm in regular email contact with Bruce Eccles and Larry Lewis. You remember those guys?"

"Yeah, those two clowns. What're they up to?"

"Larry's in Cornwall at the moment. He's set up a cleaning firm there with his cousin. And Bruce – Bruce is bit of thespian now."

"Acting the clown?"

"More behind the scenes. Like a stage manager."

"How's your brother?"

"He's fine, man. He's in Florida. In fact, it's where I'm off to now."

He glanced down at my luggage. "So you really need to make this flight," he observed.

"I'd say." I glanced in the direction of the destination board. "And I'm not sure I'm liking what I see."

"It's going to be one of those days."

With his open-stance posture and easy manner, he gave off an air of serenity that made the frantic desperation I felt inside seem childish.

"If I was going to the airport," he offered distractedly, "I would have taken a taxi."

"Well, we were in a cab," I told him. "We took in some theatre last night and we stayed over at a hotel. We don't live in London any more, see. We got up early and we'd got as far as Piccadilly in the taxi when the radio told us that something had happened further down and the queue was backing up for a couple of kilometres."

"Did they say what had happened?"

"No. But I told the wife we should get out while we were next to a tube station and get the underground to Heathrow. Even the cabbie had to admit it was the best thing. But no, she wanted to press on in the taxi. Snob, see. We hadn't moved for ten minutes, but she figured things were going to improve as we got closer to Heathrow!"

He smiled absently, then he glanced up at the destination board. Recollection of the recent incident had caused me to lose my cool again.

"You married?" I asked him.

"No."

I need not have asked. There was something about his aspect that spelt bachelordom. There was nothing unkempt about him. But he wore the expression of a man who lived selfishly.

"Significant other?" I ventured.

"Significant other?" he repeated. "Man, you sound like a little functionary!" Then, "Where'd you meet your wife?" he asked somewhat abruptly, looking at me directly for the first time.

"In uni."

"Yeah?"

"It's Brenda."

He looked momentarily puzzled.

"You know – Brenda? The American?"

Recollection broke across his face. He paused, momentarily distracted by a group of youths – two of Afro-Caribbean origin and one white – who had begun a rapping battle and who at the close of each bar of sixteen would break into excited, whooping sounds. Then he glanced my way again.

"So, you married Brenda?"

"Yeah, and I sent you an invitation, too!"

"You did?"

"I most certainly did. I'd lost your email address, so I put it through your parents' letterbox."

"I'd moved house by then," he informed me. "When did you guys get hitched?"

"Three years ago now."

"Three years? Probably wasn't even in the country then." He paused for a moment. "So you married Brenda," he mused. He opened his khaki bag again. "Well, that's a turn-up," he observed. "You happy?"

"I'd say," I replied promptly. "Are you surprised?"

"That you're happy?"

"No – that I married Brenda."

He thought about it. "Well, yeah, I am surprised."

There could only have been two answers to my question, but I wasn't ready for that one. Perhaps it showed on my face. "Why is that?" I asked.

He pulled out his plastic Coke bottle. "Why?"

"Yeah, why?"

"I just thought you'd have had better judgement," he continued.

I glared at him as I considered his words. He wasn't smiling. He brought the Coke bottle to his mouth and drank lustily this time, as if he had a real thirst. As he threw his head back, I noticed a tiny shaving cut above his bobbing Adam's apple.

"Steady," I warned. "I'm pissed off with her, but I did say she was my wife."

He paused and reflected. "What I remember most clearly about Brenda", he said, "is that time in the Sports Café – just down the road there on Haymarket. Remember that?"

I was trying to.

"Exams were early that year. I'd just finished mine and you had a couple more to do, I think. But we were all out in the Sports Café that night. I remember there were loads of Yanks there, as well. And the beer was a pound a pint or something ridiculous like that. But anyway, at one point that night the DJ stopped the music and pointed to the little stage in front of the dance floor. Do you remember that night now?"

"It was the week before some rugby cup final."

"So, you remember the DJ got one of the Wasps players to sit on a three-legged stool in the middle of the stage and invited four girls to come up on the stage. He said the one who gave the Wasp player the best lap dance would get ten tickets for the final that Sunday."

"Yeah, I remember."

"I mean, this was the time when I used to drink. And I'd drunk quite a bit that night. And I think we'd prodded all the girls to get up there on the stage. But among our group only Sadie and your girl Brenda actually got up there. I mean, she bowled right up there and she wasn't even into the sport."

9

"And?" I felt a tide of anger rise within me. I knew that he knew that four years ago, even an insinuation of the kind just made would have put him in traction for a week. He wouldn't have dared even think something like that. Was he trying to show me how there'd been a shift in the balance of power since he got himself a new-look physique? But he continued.

"I just couldn't get over how much like a ho she acted."

I made an inward promise to myself to remain calm. "I can't recall you turning down the tickets when she won," I reminded him after a moment. "In fact, if I remember correctly, you were a right pig with the champagne in the VIP on finals day. A right pig!"

"Yes," he reflected. "And that day you were the pimp. Come final reckoning," he drawled, "we'll both find none of us covered ourselves in glory that night and on that day in the so-called VIP section."

When I examined his face, there was no hint of combativeness or malevolence. His tone had been measured and reflective, as if he was merely giving voice to a very personal memory. All the while, his clear brown eyes had been distant and unfocused. I felt I couldn't take offence.

"Lighten up," I urged him. "It was a bit of fun. She was drunk that night. As we all were."

"I call it sexual titillation for pecuniary gain," he said absently. "I thought then that her actions that night said more about her character than a million empty conversations could have."

"Sexual titillation for pecuniary gain," I repeated. The phrase sounded odd to me. "So, who sounds like a little functionary now?" I asked him. "Besides, if you remember

Brenda at all, she was less in need of pecuniary gain than any of us – including the guy she was dancing for."

It had been a while, but the more he spoke, the more he filled in the details of the impression I had of him. And the more memories came to me.

I'd only once visited the home he shared with his parents in Whitechapel. He must have been sixteen at the time. I was doing my brother a favour. And at great risk to myself. My brother had lent him his GCSE Physics notes, but the exam was in a matter of days and now he wanted them returned. So I was sent to get them back. Thing was, he was alone at home, bed-ridden with chickenpox.

He had opened the door for me himself. His parents were at work and I followed him back into his bedroom. I'd gone there during my lunch break and it had been a clear summer afternoon. Light poured from the opening in the curtains and on to his unmade single bed in the far corner of the room. I'd made up my mind that I was going to be polite, and that I would simply get the notes and jet out. But he had other ideas. His enforced isolation had been giving him grief and he'd put some work into researching my entertainment. Or perhaps it didn't take that much to establish that any teenager would find it hard to pull away from computer games, chocolates and DVDs.

I felt he was lucky to have a room of his own. At the time I was still sharing with my brother. He told me his three sisters shared the bedroom opposite and that no one, not even his parents, dared walk in here without his permission. All the while I was trying to keep as much distance between us as is possible between two people sharing a ten-by-ten space.

On the walls were plastered posters of Bollywood actresses and female R&B performers. I'd been mildly surprised by those girl posters, because I'd never seen him make a move on any of the girls we knew. When I'd told my brother about what I'd seen, he'd put it more poetically. He reckoned Monster was the type who rather than get cracking with what was to hand – would instead wank to images of perfection from distant lands.

I'd spent the whole afternoon with him. During that time, I counted exactly forty-three Monster Munch crisp packets in his room. I came across these packets on his bookshelf, between DVD covers, on the floorboards and strewn across his bed. In any case, on that day was born the nickname that was to stick with him through school, then university and – who knows? – later on in life.

"Monster," I said to him. "At uni I thought you were improving. But, really, you sound more of a miserable bastard than you did back at school."

"Jonah," he smiled. "We've been talking for minutes. You know nothing of my life now."

Despite what he'd said, the longer I stood there, the more of an inexplicable attraction I felt towards him and his new laid-back confidence. Maybe it was the current uncertainty about my life that made me more sentimental about people and places from a more stable period. "So, what about you, Monst?" I asked him. "Have you found fulfilment?"

While he seemed to think about it, his expression took

on a resigned cast. "Not yet," he confided. And then, with his left hand, using thumb and index finger, he indicated the length of a fingernail. "But I'm this close." He smiled, and his teeth were an uncommon white.

"Well, that's good for you," I told him.

It was then that I voiced the crazy idea of inviting him to our next reunion. "We're taking a floor in the Connaught in Bournemouth. Why don't you come down? As a surprise guest. I'm sure everyone will be pleased to see you."

He was staring into some indeterminate space beyond me. "Are you serious?"

"Why not?"

He shook his head. "Can't make it then."

I shrugged. "That's too bad," I said.

"And neither can you," he promptly added.

His matter-of-fact tone surprised me. "Well, I might not make this flight today . . ." I began. He interrupted. "No, you're not going to make it, Jonah."

I examined his face. As with his first comment about Brenda, he wasn't smiling. He continued. "Because right here between my legs" – my gaze went down to his Adidas sports bag – "is nine pounds of explosive."

He slowly lifted the sports bag to his chest. You may not have the resolution on your camera to see this, but protruding from the zipper was a drawstring about a metre long. "And when I pull this here," he added, "most will say goodbye, and one or two, hello."

I zoomed in on that bag and it became magnified to the size of a small vehicle in my eyes. I knew right then he wasn't kidding. Monster had moments of wit. But practical jokes had never been his thing. A chill ran through every muscle and sinew of my body. I dared not take my eyes off him and his bag. You will see that, from the time he said those words, the bag become the centre of my universe. He remained expressionless though, save for his eyes, which were tiny circles of pure, determined evil. I got queasy as the realisation intensified that right here – within minutes, perhaps – I was going to meet my end.

In my peripheral view I noticed more people had come through on to the platform. The rappers had moved down and background noise was now coming from a group of football fans in Spurs shirts. I averted my eyes for a fraction of a second and glanced down the platform. The last thing I wanted was to put his nerves on edge.

"I bet now you wish you hadn't stopped to say hello," he suggested.

"Would it have made a difference?" I asked. I was surprised at how calmly my words rolled out.

"I suppose not."

I was relieved that he was continuing to speak. Somehow uttering these words eased the nerves. It lent just a touch of normality to this crazy situation where, unknown to the rest of the platform, a man raised in multicultural London and schooled in modern science had mutated into a fanatic intent on blowing up them and a former schoolmate in the name of religion. He still seemed calm and contained.

A gust of wind and a collective gasp of anticipation signalled the arrival of the Heathrow-bound train. I turned and saw the lights come into view. For me, they were as welcome as the yellow eyes of a lungeing predator.

"Al," I said, calling him by his proper name for the first time, "I'm asking you to let me go."

His mouth tightened. "I can't," he began. The roar of the incoming train blanked the rest of his words, but I expect he voiced some crap about not wanting to risk spoiling the plans of people who were depending on him. He positioned himself behind me. He prodded me to pick up my luggage and to step forward. He knew elbows and shoulders would soon get to work as the doomed crowd, now ten deep, began jockeying for position before the yellow line that ran the length of the platform. He was directing me well. I was moving in the slipstream of a broad-backed and purposeful football supporter. Progress was halted by the lucky lot getting off the train. My demeanour must have been like that of a guy being led to the gallows.

There was no chance of finding a seat. I moved as far as I could into the carriage. Then I dropped my bags and turned to face the open door. Monster positioned himself alongside me and we watched the mad scramble of those still trying to squeeze themselves in before the doors closed. An announcement came through on the platform that, for the security of passengers, CCTV was in operation at this station. Members of the public were urged to report anything or anyone who looked suspicious. I stole a glance at Monster and I swear, he smiled.

I watched with mounting nausea as the carriage filled to the point where people stood pressed chest to back up against one another. Monster's right hand gripped the handle of the sports bag. The khaki pouch had been squashed into his pocket and his left hand now grasped the drawstring. Finally, the announcement was made for passengers to stand clear of the doors. A heavy-set woman in high heels showed unlikely athleticism by making a last-second leap from the platform edge to the lip of the carriage. The doors closed on the rest of those on the platform. And so were separated the living from the soon-to-be-dead.

There followed a moment of silence, during which I watched those in groups exchange skyward glances and roll their eyes at each other at finally being able to make it on board. I looked down at one kid a metre or two in front of me. He was no more than four years old. Unable to reach a pole, he'd hooked his finger into a front belt loop of his mother's jeans. The woman was dark-haired with big brown liquid eyes. She smiled indulgently down at him. I had to avert my eyes. My thoughts turned to Brenda. Her hesitancy up there in the taxi didn't seem so ridiculous now that this ride of death was set to start.

Strangely, I also thought about that plastic Coke bottle. I imagined he'd bought it only moments earlier, in the kiosk upstairs. And this concern of his, for the temporary comforts of a body he was soon to rip apart with explosive, freaked me out. Strangely, I speculated whether in his pockets he still carried change from that last transaction and in what denominations. There was a moment when only the tinny sounds of music on iPod headphones reached my ears. Soon, even those sounds would be replaced by eternal silence. And the ridiculousness of my situation came through to me with a sickening clarity. There I'd been, manfully palming away the slings and arrows of life in the belief they were but minor irritants on the road to some as yet ill-defined but ultimately worthy, if not glorious end. It turned out that this was it. This was the purpose – to get my insides blown away on the Piccadilly Line by a former schoolmate. To become a statistic in a news report – a negative statistic for my people, but a positive statistic for many others. So, not even just a statistic, but a statistic of variable emotive pull.

But, once marked for imminent death, the mind can turn to ridiculously practical matters. I gathered Monster would never allow me distance enough to shout the alarm and yet get away safely. So, I resolved to remain close enough to him to make it as quick and painless an end as I could. Even then, I knew there would be nothing worse than copping the kind of impact that would have you hovering back and forth in a narrow realm between severely maimed and almost dead, but only to fall, after long and medieval suffering, on the wrong side of the divide.

The train made a start again. Then a second later, just as suddenly, it stopped, sending passengers crashing into each other and setting off a chorus of tut-tuttings. The door opened again. A suited youngster took the chance to hop on. Again, the doors closed.

Suddenly impotence and a rising rage threatened to overwhelm me. I glanced at Monster, and for the first time his expression had lost its serenity. A coating of sweat now covered his forehead. He was fidgeting. We exchanged nervous glances. My temples throbbed. The driver then announced that the train would be going out of service owing to a fault with the doors. Customers were advised to wait until the next train. Monster prodded me to step off.

The way I chose to read it was that something, some force of mercy, had presented me with a window of reprieve. I took it as a sign. Now, it was up to me to make use of it.

"It's not the way, you know," I told him when I was back on the platform with the other iPod-wearing, disgruntled commuters. "You know what I mean," I continued, as his eyes scanned the platform. He had become even more edgy and fidgety.

"No, I don't know what you mean," he said, without looking at me.

"Violence as an instrument of change," I continued. "Violence as a means to challenge authority."

"No?"

"People who read of what happens here will only harden their hearts against you guys. That'll be the only outcome of all this. That's why I say using violence against people and situations you don't like is not the way to go here."

He spoke without looking into my eyes. "I ought to shoot you just for saying that," he threatened.

I hadn't thought that he was armed. "Well, if that's the way you feel."

"It takes a man of major stupidity to clock up all these hours in history lessons and not learn that violence has shaped history more than anything else ever could. Nothing significant and lasting gets done other than through violence or the threat of violence," he whispered hoarsely.

I had the feeling that it was a relief for him to speak

like this, and that he was only indulging me on this level to help ease his own nerves and strengthen his fading resolve. So I kept talking.

"My honest view, Al, is that stuff like medical science, industrialisation, air travel, have shaped what and where we are now, more than violence ever did." All the while my glance kept switching from his sweaty face to that bag he carried.

He was staring straight ahead. But I knew I had to reach the skinny, R&B-loving, Monster Munch-chomping kid that I knew was still in there somewhere.

"You've got innocent people all around you," I noted. "Look."

"You're resorting to cliché. It must be the pressure."

"The proof is all around. There are kids here!"

"And there were kids over there. What's in a few kilometres if it's morality we're talking?"

He fixed me with a challenging stare and I knew then that there would be no reasoning with him. But I felt I had to keep him talking.

"It's become fashionable to speak ill of violent methods," he said distractedly. "It's lazy thinking, though. Because when you have fixed opposing views and the stakes are high, it's the only way to get through. Always has been."

The destination board said two minutes till the next train. "Look, man," I said. My voice had gone high-pitched and tremulous. "I've got nothing personal against anyone. We all live in this society together. Whatever the rights and wrongs, can I ask you as a man – if not as a friend, then as a person who has a shared past with you – to delay just twenty minutes?"

"No can do." He did not look at me when he said this.

"Not for my sake. But I've got a son, man. A three-year-old son." I could hear my voice failing me, cracking up.

But his face wasn't giving anything away. "You never said that before," he said. "Want to appeal to my sentimentality? You think there's any in there?" His tone wasn't promising much.

"That's not the issue."

"Where is he now?"

"He's coming along with his mother."

He glanced at the destination board. "Yeah, right."

"I told you I'd left them in the taxi in the hope she'd eventually follow my lead and come down. She should be here any minute."

"And how'd you know they're not here yet?"

"They'd have to come through this entrance and I would have seen them. I've been watching."

"How old did you say your boy was?"

"Three. In July he'll be four."

I watched his eyes. He paused. "Mine's two and a half," he said.

So that was that. He glanced at his watch. The destination board now said one minute till the Heathrow train. I made up my mind then that I wasn't going to have salvage and restoration crews hosing my guts and liver from the insides of the carriage whose doors opened before me. I owed it to my son to at least to go down fighting. With a renewed sense of purpose, I picked up my bags and shuffled my way to the edge of the platform. Monster moved slowly behind me and drew alongside. I knew what I had to do.

When the train comes into view, I kept telling myself, *I lean towards him and mouth some words without actually saying anything. Thinking that my words have been blanked by the sound of the coming train, he leans closer toward me. I lean towards him, making out to repeat what I said, and then in one bold move I shove the bastard on to the path of the oncoming train.*

"OK. That's enough," announces an authoritative voice. It's the guy who came late into the control room.

I'm uncertain what to do next. I turn my neck, and with the circular motion of his finger he gives me the OK to turn my seat around to face them. *He's very tall and thin – more college professor than detective,* I say to myself. His eyes take in my bruised stomach and chest, and his smile is almost apologetic as he introduces himself.

"I'm Damien," he says. Alongside him sits the female officer and the guys who pummelled me earlier as I tried to force my way out of the underground station and into the open air.

"If this is some kind of interrogation . . ." I begin. "Because there's no time."

Damien shakes his head. "No interrogation, Mr Martins," he says. "You volunteered your version of events."

"Version of events?"

He shrugs as if, despite his best efforts, that's what it remains to him.

There's a knock on the door and Damien leaves his seat to see who it is. He returns with a sheet of paper clipped between his long fingers. An air of expectancy fills the room as he reads it in silence. But then he places it in the inside pocket of his jacket without a glance towards the rest of us.

"You were dead keen to hang on to that mobile phone, too," he observes.

"I wanted to call my wife. I still want to talk to her. Can I use a telephone?"

He shook his head.

"As you'll find out pretty soon," I tell him, "my luggage is harmless. I left it on the platform only to get up those stairs more quickly. When your tests are done, you'll find nothing in there but gifts, clothing, some jewellery."

"What our guys are going to struggle with later is why someone intent on a mission like this would choose to let you go before he got on the train."

"I have no idea why. It wasn't anything to do with sentiment, though. Maybe he thought I was jinxing him."

"That you were jinxing him?" he repeated.

"I'm just saying. Perhaps."

In silence, all eyes turn to the monitors now showing a live picture of my two items of luggage sitting on the empty tube platform.

THE MONEY SHOT

Bruce and the photographer sit in a shiny black BMW SUV. The windows are heavily tinted and they are parked on Air Street, opposite the nightclub, Chinawhite.

It's a warm September night and they've been in the vehicle for half an hour so far. They've swapped places so that the photographer is now in the driver's seat facing the entrance to the club, and Bruce shifts restlessly in the passenger seat. The passenger door opens to a wall that runs the length of the street.

The photographer fidgets with the strap of his Pentax K100D. It protrudes from between his wide-open thighs like some long, fat phallus. He senses that Bruce is nervous and, perhaps to lighten the mood, he poses a question.

"Of all these jocks around at the moment," he asks – and he pauses – "which one would you swap places with?"

"How long have you been in England?" Bruce asks in turn. "Here we call them sports personalities. We don't ever call them jocks."

"Whatever. But who would you swap places with for a year?"

Bruce appears to think about it for half a minute, then

he mumbles that he'd have a couple of years as Tiger Woods – perhaps.

"The golfer. Oh yeah?"

"If it was on offer, yeah."

"Why him?"

"Because he's the kind of guy who can just go out there and do what he has to do. His destiny is in his own hands. Not like a forward having to depend so much on his midfield or a running back having to depend so much on his quarterback and vice versa. On the course, no one can mess up for Tiger Woods apart from Tiger Woods himself."

Bruce's phone goes off. He answers after the second ring. It's the tenth call in as many minutes. He doesn't need to check the display to know that it's the newspaper editor again. Bruce keeps the phone to his ear in silence for a long time before taking a deep breath.

"How many times have I seen you right with this type of thing?" he exhales in a peevish tone. He listens again. "If that's going to make you feel any better," he continues. "And if it's going to get you off the phone every second, why don't you? Why don't you send your man down? Tell him we're in a black SUV off Air Street!" He rings off.

Within twenty minutes, they hear a tap on the side of the vehicle. The photographer winds the window down and a cleanly shaven twenty-something introduces himself as Stevie. He says he works for the paper and he pulls a yellow laminated card from his back pocket and flashes it before their eyes. The photographer waves him to the side door, but Stevie says he wants to get a burger first. He asks whether they want anything. They decline, and so Stevie trundles off to the McDonald's at the end of the street.

Bruce glances down at his watch. He sighs. He's restless. The arrangement of tin cans, magazines and empty milkshake cartons around his feet gets realigned as he stretches and yawns. Soraya was supposed to call Bruce at eleven o'clock with an update. The photographer knows this. He suggests to Bruce that he call her. Bruce blows out his cheeks while scrolling down for her number. He dials and waits.

"How many exits to this place?" the photographer asks.

"Definitely the one," says Bruce. Then, "Damn it!" he snaps.

"What's up?" the photographer asks him.

"Her phone's turned off."

"Maybe she's getting busy early," teases the photographer.

Bruce remains poker-faced. "She knows the score," he assures himself.

"What're you going to do?"

Bruce rubs his chin. "Let's see."

There are footsteps and Stevie returns. He knocks on the photographer's window, then passes around the back. As he slides in, using the door facing the wall, Bruce warns him not to sit on the computer notebook they've set up on the back seat. Stevie wears jeans, brown boots and a blue striped shirt. Bruce has remained strong in the face of scores of requests from his photographer companion to turn the radio on. In the silence, the sound of Stevie munching through his burger and fries comes through loudly.

"No way for a young dude to spend a Saturday night, really, is it?" comments the photographer after a moment. "Where were you?"

His question catches Stevie mid-swallow. "I was at a party," he replies, as he taps his chest gently with his fist. Then he returns to his munching.

"Everything OK back there?" Bruce asks after a while.

"Sure," replies Stevie.

"Did your man brief you?"

"Soraya Ellman is in the club, right? And she's supposed to be coming out with Ray Pollinger at twelve fifteen, right?"

"That's the plan," says Bruce.

"And how's it going?"

Bruce glances up at the rear-view mirror and catches Stevie's eyes. "Everything's cool," he solemnly tells him. Then, after a pause, "But we need to monitor things – to make sure it stays that way."

"Of course. Sure."

The photographer comments on how the smell of burgers and fries has worked up an appetite in him. Stevie offers to get him a Big Mac.

Bruce has an idea, though. "Hey, Stevie," he asks. "Can you go down and see if she's OK? You know what she looks like, don't you?"

The request catches Stevie by surprise. "Yeah, I know what Soraya looks like," he stutters.

"Finish your grub first, though, man."

"I'm done," says Stevie, his mouth still full. He makes a show of scrunching the paper wrapper loudly in hands. "Where shall I put this?"

Bruce stretches his arm and takes the wrapper from Stevie. He holds it for a while in his palm, then deposits it at his feet along with the rest of the rubbish.

The second after Stevie closes the passenger door behind him, the photographer turns to Bruce. "Good-looking boy, ain't he?"

"I wouldn't leave him alone with the wife."

"But was it a good call to send him down there?

"Why not?" questions Bruce.

"Why not? I mean, more than likely he'll just call his boss and that'll only make the guy more worried that we've got problems here. Meaning more grief for you."

"I need to know what's going on," says Bruce.

There's a knock on the side of the driver's door. The photographer winds the window down. It's Stevie again.

"They won't let me in," he complains. "I need to be on the guest list."

Bruce reaches into his pocket and pulls out a wodge of notes. He passes them to the photographer, who then shoves them into Stevie's hands. The photographer leaves the window wound down and they watch Stevie take the short queue. This time, he breezes past the red velvet ropes and descends into the club. Bruce glances at his watch. It's 11.20 p.m. The photographer winds the window up.

Stevie returns ten minutes later and climbs into the back seat. "She's on a table with Ray, another guy and six other girls," he tells them.

"Is she pissed?" asks the photographer.

"Looks more pissed off than pissed."

"What's the other guy look like?

"Really tall guy. Not a footballer. One of Ray's hangers-on, perhaps. Anything the matter?"

"Not really," replies Bruce. "We're on schedule, but

earlier we asked her to call us every quarter of an hour. And she hasn't been doing that."

"Oh," says Stevie. "But there's no reception down there."

"There isn't?" questions Bruce.

"Nope. I tried making a call myself."

"Bruce was worried she'd already passed out down there," explains the photographer.

"No, she's up and around," confirms Stevie.

"What team do you support, Stevie?" Bruce suddenly asks.

"I'm not into football."

"So you've got no issue shopping a West Ham player? No moral issue?"

Stevie shakes his head.

"That's good," Bruce tells him. "Because I'm a West Ham man myself. But I've got no respect for a guy who could let his team mates down when the rest of them are making sacrifices."

Stevie says nothing. The photographer begins whistling a nursery rhyme.

"I don't want to be funny," begins Bruce, "but you know you said you tried to make a call when you were down there?"

"Yeah?"

"Well, it wasn't to our man, was it?"

Steve shakes his head. "No. It was a private call."

Bruce points to the photographer. "Because, in his part of the world, they'd say your boss has been busting our balls over this project."

"Really?"

"Big time."

"It's a huge story," comments Stevie.

"And it's under control," Bruce adds solemnly. He pauses, then smiles. "But if it came from you that it was under control, it wouldn't half make our lives easier."

Stevie laughs. It's a nervous laugh.

"But hey, Stevie," continues Bruce. "Seriously, we need to get a message to this girl. We need to get the state of play from her. Can you go back down there and ask her to come up for a cigarette, so we can talk to her again?"

Stevie looks momentarily puzzled, but despite himself he agrees to go back into the club. He leaves via the door that gives on to the wall. They watch him flash his ink-stamped wrist at the security guy. The velvet rope is lifted over his head and he descends into the club again.

After a moment, Bruce's phone goes off. It's the editor again. He wants to speak to Stevie.

"Call him in fifteen minutes," snaps Bruce. Then suddenly, in a much more agreeable tone, "It's all good here. Don't worry." The second he clicks off, Bruce smacks the heel of his palm against his forehead theatrically.

"You can understand his position, can't you?" offers the photographer.

Bruce says nothing. His fingers close around the middle button of his shirt and he tugs five times in quick succession while puffing out his cheeks.

"But you can see where he's coming from?" the photographer repeats.

"No, I can't," insists Bruce. "I've given this guy dozens of stories over the years."

"The story's already written, but if it's going to run on Sunday morning, Soraya needs to get Ray into a state where he's walking out of that front door with her by midnight. Now, I'm not sure what she's said to you, but that sounds tough to me. And if the story doesn't run tonight, it loses its punch, and it's not the kind of story you can run without the photo. Past reputation counts for nothing with stakes like that."

"Past reputation is everything."

"Bruce, what I'm saying is I'd be worried if I was counting on a Sunday exclusive front page, hoping to clinch it within one hour and the whole thing was hanging on promises made by some drugged-up and dizzy socialite soccer groupie. Now, all I'm saying is if you were in that position, then you'd definitely be nervy, too."

Bruce snorts derisively. "Is he the only one? We all stand to get busted if this doesn't play out. It'll hurt all of us – reputationally and financially."

"Is she really that close to this Ray?" asks the photographer. "I thought she was into older guys, anyway. And even if she did fuck him on Wednesday – tonight he might be looking for something fresh. He might be moving on. You know how these guys do it!"

"I've been in this game long enough to know when I've got something. This ain't the first tip-off Soraya's given me."

The photographer laughs.

"Besides," adds Bruce, "you're wrong about her."

"What part am I wrong about?"

He looks away from his colleague. "You know, dizzy, drugged-up, socialite, blonde?" he sniffs.

"Yeah? What part of all that is wrong?"

"The only correct bit was the physical description," says Bruce, tugging at the front of his shirt again. He pauses for a moment. "Like, did you know she's an Anthropology graduate?"

The photographer smiles. "She told you that?"

"You talk to Stevie when he gets back."

"Yeah, right."

"She's a graduate. But you won't find that on her Facebook page. She gives off the image she wants people like you to see. She knows what she's doing."

"Excuse me, but I heard she started lapdancing at eighteen. Don't know where the degree fitted in with all that."

"Started working in Spearmint Rhino when she was an undergraduate. If you're a blonde, slim, six-foot-tall woman in London, people will approach you to do that kind of work. Hard to turn down when waitressing, selling magazine space or working in retail for the minimum wage are the other options."

"I'm not sure."

"Thing with Soraya is, she got greedy. Money was good, so she carried on far too long. Even after she graduated. Then she fell into glamour modelling and everything that goes with that."

"Nothing wrong with glamour modelling."

Bruce turns reflective. "But she wants out from all that now," he explains. "She's grown up. This little caper with Ray down there – it's her swansong, I reckon."

"Her exit package?"

"That's what I reckon."

The photographer peers through the tinted windows. The queue outside the club has increased fourfold in the past twenty minutes. A black van approaches and a tension-filled silence falls as the two men brace themselves for the appearance of a rival predator on the scene. The van slows on its approach, but then picks up speed after passing the club entrance.

"So she should be digging for mummies in Egypt," continues the photographer, picking up the thread of their earlier conversation. "That's what she should be doing. Not looking for sugar daddies in London, or digging for gold in the pockets of married soccer captains in night-clubs. Right?"

Bruce casts him an incredulous look. A shriek of laughter rises from nearby. He glances at the rear-view mirror. A mixed group of smokers have congregated behind the vehicle. "I said she was an anthropologist. An anthropologist. Not a fucking archaeologist, dummy."

"Whatever."

Stevie hesitates on his way down. Who would have thought these faux-marble steps, grey-looking in the dim light and some chipped at the edges, led down to one of the plushest of London's nightclubs? Perhaps management kept the entrance basic, the better to stun first-time entrants with the Middle Eastern opulence they met once they got down those stairs. He's more used to and comfortable with the grittier clubs and bars in the Shoreditch area. More importantly, he's used to being in the company of his girlfriend or his mates in this type of social setting.

So, as he makes his way past the cloakroom, he's accompanied by a sense of mild anxiety. This follows him even after he grabs his whisky and Coke and retreats from the pulsing bar area. He's buffeted by shoulders and palms and he's unsure where to position himself. He settles on a spot near a row of cushion-covered banquettes facing the staircase. But no more than a minute standing there alone has him feeling like a cop. Worse still, he feels that, very soon, everyone else will think he's some kind of undercover cop, too.

It now crosses his mind that, before agreeing to make direct contact with Soraya, he ought perhaps to have cleared it first with the boss. He makes a rolling motion with his neck as if to dislodge that unbidden and awkward notion from his head. He then glances at his watch to verify how forty minutes remain for Soraya to get Ray out of that front door.

Ray's group is holding court on a table positioned at the back of the club. Stevie quickly determines that his challenge is to keep an eye out for Soraya's movements while avoiding Ray's gaze. Ray now has a raging antipathy towards journalists, or people he even suspects of being journalists. He refused to speak to the press for eighteen months after GQ announced to the world his supposed belief that Addis Ababa was an Italian designer of gentlemen's suits. Stuff like that was swallowed by scores of nouveau riche celebrities every year without much fuss. But Ray gets sensitive about his East London education. His vow of silence lasted as long as it took for him to catch up with the writer. The scene was the lobby of the Dorchester after the *South Bank Show* awards. The writer suffered a broken jaw. Money exchanged hands, key witnesses succumbed to amnesia and the prosecution's case folded.

As much as sections of the sports press bemoan his inconsistency on the field, Ray Pollinger is remarkably consistent regarding the type of women he chooses to be seen with. A busty Romanian brunette call girl once sold a story about him, but apart from that, if a keen biographer arrayed photographs of Ray's past partners, he'd seem to have a profile of a man on a personal mission to run through the female line of a single, tall, slim-ankled, blonde and narrow-hipped Teutonic family.

Following his wedding to an ex-choreographer two years ago, Ray's profile on the gossip pages has decreased significantly. Every weekday, on the final kick of his training session, he retreats behind the doors of his mock-Tudor mansion to his computer games and his young family, and he won't be seen till his Aston Martin pulls away from his drive on its way to the ground for the next session.

Stevie has always found that, without any alcohol in his system, the beat and throb of this type of nightclub music only serves to put him in an irritable mood. He is now keen to move to a more secluded spot in the club. As he wends his way towards the bar again, he notices that some people are seated behind that main bar. If he can count on those coming to the main bar to be concentrating on getting served rather than looking beyond, it's a good spot from which to catch Soraya when eventually she makes a dash for the bathroom.

From his vantage point, Stevie gives some thought to the Soraya question. Drink in hand, and eyes on the dancing crowd, he considers why she hasn't provided Bruce with the promised updates. A few possibilities come to mind. She could simply have forgotten. Or perhaps, she found she couldn't get a phone signal and then she got distracted. Another more worrying possibility is that Ray may have charmed her since her last conversation with Bruce and she may have changed her mind about the deal. In that case, great care will have to be taken with his opening line to her.

Ray's friend walks past – unaccompanied. Stevie thinks he's Albanian. He's very tall, though, and as he moves his head is a periscope above the bobbing crowd of dancers. He passes in the direction of the exit and the bathroom. His head is less animated on his way back to the group. He now has three miniskirted girls in tow and Stevie notices how he moves with a slight limp.

A minute later, a guy in a pinstripe suit slaps his similarly clad friend on the shoulder to alert him to the passage of one of the finer specimens of womanhood in the club. It's Soraya, striding through the crowd. Stevie dashes down the short steps running along the side of the bar, and by the time she gains the stairs leading to the exit he is right behind her. Instead of heading to the bathroom, as he expects, she turns left into another room. The room is smaller and less densely packed than the main dance floor. Here, couples recline against gold-brocaded, tasselled, fat cushions, sipping champagne and periodically cupping their hands around each other's diamond-encrusted ears. Others smooch on the floor. Champagne glass in hand, Soraya pauses in the centre of the room. Stevie slides further in, then he gives her his back as he pretends to address the DJ positioned in the corner. After a moment, he steals a sneaky glance over his shoulder in time to watch her blow out two guys who approach her with a line. He watches her stare at her mobile phone. While he ponders his next move, she exits the room. She's now heading for the bathroom. Bouncing on his toes, he waits for her to emerge. When she does, he intercepts her by grabbing her hand.

"Hi," he says.

In a millisecond, she scans him head to hip with her large, pale blue eyes. "You haven't got a drink," she observes.

His heart races. He relaxes his grip. "I had one."

"Well, let me get you another." She smiles, grabs his hand, and she's off in the direction of the main dance floor.

He tugs back. He wants to talk right here, in the quietest spot in the club. But her grip is deceptively strong and she's well on the move now. It does not escape him how much more readily the dancing crowd parts for her than it did for him minutes earlier when he followed her. Within seconds, he finds himself before a low table, whose surface is almost totally obscured by bottles, glasses and ice buckets. About fifteen people are standing or remain seated around this table, their faces periodically illumined by the fluorescent straws carried aloft by the nimble-footed waitresses who scurry back and forth from the bar. Ray is seated at the far end. His eyes are cast downward while a bejewelled blonde whispers into his ear.

The opening bars of a tune come through and a roar goes out from the crowd. Some rise from their seats. Stevie looks up, then he takes a quick glance behind him. He's surrounded by women nursing champagne flutes between their manicured fingers and swaying to the rhythm of the music. Soraya grins at him. She reaches over and, without asking what he wants to drink or whether he's driving, pours him a glass of champagne.

He raises his glass to her beaming face, then brings it to his lips. "Who are you here with?" he begins.

She points to Ray. "With my friend," she tells him, allowing her index finger to linger there in Ray's direction. "He's having a rough time lately, so I'm looking after him a bit." Ray lifts his head in time to catch her eye. He then switches his gaze briefly to Stevie and raises his glass. Stevie smiles back.

Soraya turns to Stevie. "You alright, babes?"

"Do you want to get him up for a cigarette?" asks Stevie as he nods in the direction of Ray.

"I don't smoke," she responds. "Neither does he."

Conversation might be difficult enough without the music and the hubbub. But her eyes keep darting around the room. He has to touch her arm to get her attention every time he wants to say something. He senses her anxiety, too. Then, suddenly, she rises and beckons to the tall guy, who walks with the limp. She pulls down his shoulder to whisper into his ear. They talk animatedly. She seems to be complaining to him about something. But they keep talking into each other's ears, and above the music Stevie can't make out what they're saying. It's clear, however, that she's doing most of the talking and he keeps shrugging his shoulders or gently patting the back of her neck. The corners of his mouth are turned down.

Then the tall guy limps away from the table. He scans the room as he heads towards the exit. It's about the third time Stevie has seen him do this. Stevie figures that, like the waitresses, this guy has an irrigation role; that while the waitresses replenish Ray's table with top-quality alcohol, the tall guy in like manner replenishes the area with attractive women. The composition of the outer circles and inner circles near the table keeps changing as a stream of mini-skirted, midriff-baring women move in to replace those whose time near the star has lapsed and who've been found lacking as entertainment. The waste management aspect of the role is carried out with considerably less charm and aplomb. Timed-out beauties are eased from their seats and gently shouldered back to the outer circles of the table. Some hang around, some seek irrigation elsewhere – more gentlemanly tables to decorate.

"You alright, babes?" asks Soraya.

She's playing the bimbo, Stevie says to himself. *No one gets a first in Anthropology and talks the way she does.* He glances over at Ray. The guy has a wine glass in his hand. He's also holding the close attention of another woman now – a redhead wearing black sunglasses. Stevie wonders what Ray and Soraya talk about when they're together without their court attendants around them. He wonders whether they're still together.

"I'm fine, darling," Stevie tells her. If she wants to keep it light, he could keep it even lighter. But, in any case, he has to get her outside soon.

Moments later, she's distracted again. Stevie follows her eye line and notices that Ray is now looming over them. Stevie's heart does a leap.

"Now, who's this drinking my champagne?" demands Ray, full glass dangling precariously close to the edge of his fingers.

Soraya grins and introduces the men to each other. Ray examines Stevie's face, then narrows his eyes.

"I've seen you before, ain't I?"

Stevie's heart is still racing.

"On a shoot somewhere," Ray continues. "You a model, yeah?"

"No," says Stevie, relieved not to have been sniffed out.

"What do you do?" Ray asks flatly. He's unsteady on his feet.

"Royal Air Force," replies Stevie. It was the first thing that came into his head.

"You on R&R?"

Stevie nods.

"Where from?"

"Afghanistan."

A slow smile spreads over Ray's face. "Yeah? Definitely haven't seen you, then. Who you with tonight?"

"I've come here on my own."

He grins. "Well, you're not alone now! That's cool. You're in good hands." Ray winks. "Enjoy!" He clinks his glass against Stevie's and wanders unsteadily back to his spot at the table.

Stevie glances at his watch. He has to get Soraya out of there. It crosses his mind to ask her straight out what her position is with Bruce. But Ray's recent little action has complicated things. The word "entrapment" in large white lettering and set against a black background looms large in his mind. His thinking is being muddled by the whisky and the champagne, but he tries for a moment to dredge from his memory what the press Code of Conduct would say about his role in the mess he's stumbling through. Soraya slides up close now. Her eyes are glassy as she gazes at him.

"You alright, babes?"

Within a minute, it seems, a waitress clears a space on

the table and sets down a magnum of Moët. Stevie glances over at Ray, who raises his glass. Ray then turns to the blonde next to him and whispers into her ear. She heads in the direction of the DJ booth, disappearing into the crowd. Soraya draws so close that her knees are now touching Stevie's. She smiles. The next time he glances over, Ray is talking to the same young woman who disappeared into the crowd earlier. This time, Ray is raising his voice at her. She has a distressed look on her face. Then he disappears into the crowd, leaving her standing there.

Soraya crashes her knee against Stevie's thigh. He turns to her, but she says nothing. She simply smiles.

Stevie motions his head in the direction of the spot lately vacated by Ray. "Are you two going out?" he then shouts into her ear.

She smiles languidly. "Why don't you ask him?"

He shrugs.

"He wants to keep a low profile tonight," she confides.

The opening strains of an old song come booming from the speakers. It's "Unfinished Sympathy" by Massive Attack. Ray is back in his spot. He looks across and raises a toast to Stevie again.

By now, Soraya is all but climbing over Stevie and it begins to make the newspaperman nervous and uncomfortable. He tells her he's going outside to smoke a cigarette. With just minutes to go, he needs to speak to Bruce.

He gains the first of the faux-marble steps when he feels a hand on his shoulder. It's Ray.

"Where're you going?" he wants to know. "You're not leaving?"

"No, I'm going for a smoke," Stevie tells him.

Ray stares blankly back, his eyes great white saucers. "I'll come with you," he suddenly declares.

Stevie stares back. "Why not?"

"Soraya tells me you're a footballer," Stevie says, playing the innocent, after he's lit up.

Ray doesn't respond.

"Who'd you play for?"

"I captain England in a day's time – or maybe two." He shakes his head, laughing at himself.

"Wow."

"Wow, my arse. I just kick a fucking ball around."

Stevie hands him the cigarette packet. With a wave of his hand, Ray declines.

Stevie glances at the SUV. It's impossible to see what Bruce is doing behind those tinted windows.

"You know how long it is since I've been to one of those clubs?" asks Ray. In the flesh he's less imposing than he looks on the television screen.

Stevie shrugs his shoulders.

"Must be one year almost," Ray announces.

"Since you got the captaincy."

"It was nothing to do with that," he snaps. "I just got bored of the scene."

On the sound of a tooting horn, Stevie's eyes turn to the SUV. Ray points in the direction of a silver Lexus parked lower down. "It's Dan, my driver," he explains. He rubs his face with his hands, as if to wake himself up. He seems uncomfortable here outside the darkness provided by the club. In the artificial light, it's clear that he's "dressed down" in jeans and a long-sleeved white linen shirt. The only jewellery visible is the diamond stud in his left ear.

"So you're at the end of your tour?" he asks.

Stevie nods yes.

He laughs. "I'm not going ask you how many of them you've scrubbed out. I bet you get asked that all the time."

Stevie nods again and Ray smiles.

"I have sympathy with anyone who gets asked dumbass questions nearly every day of their life."

Ray is interrupted by a hand that comes across his shoulder. It's Alex Closs, the snooker player. He's with his girlfriend, the celebrity chef, Jae Phillips. He embraces Ray before making his way down the steps. Stevie has almost finished his cigarette. Ray turns to him.

"You're a humble guy, aren't you?"

Stevie shrugs. "I don't know."

"No, don't look ashamed of it. It's a good thing. A good thing, mate." He tilts his chin in the direction of the velvet rope. "Look at some of these fuckers down there. Have you spoken to many of them?"

"Not really," Stevie replies.

"Think they're the dog's bollocks because they sing a song that some old producer's knocked out for them, or because they knock up a flan on the TV or they whack a round ball over a net for a living. Yeah they fucking think they're stars because they're on the TV. But a guy like you . . ." He rests his hand on Stevie's shoulder and pulls him forward. "You risk your own life so worthless fuckers like that can even continue breathing!" His eyes are misty. He rocks on his feet as he speaks.

Just then, it crosses Stevie's mind how half the population of the country, along with his team mates, would be counting on this guy's poise and balance to keep the

German forwards at bay. Thousands of pounds would have crossed betting-shop counters in the expectation that in a matter of hours, he'd do what he was paid for, that he'd demonstrate the attributes he'd become famous for, and here he is, just hours before that World Cup qualifier, showing all the coordination of a sleepy toddler.

"I just do my thing," mumbles Stevie. He sneaks a glance at the SUV. He wonders what Bruce is making of the silent scene playing out in front of him.

"I tell you what I'm going to do," continues Ray, his head wobbling on his neck. "I tell you what I'm personally going to do when we go back down there. I'm going to demand . . . I'm going to demand that every fucker in there buys you a drink."

Stevie laughs nervously.

"No, no. I'm serious man! That's what I'm going to do. I'm not going to hear nothing about you being humble. That's what I'm going to do. I'm going to demand that every fucker in there dips into his fucking wallet and spends some of his undeserved fucking cash to stand you a drink. It's the least they can do. Then I'm gonna . . ."

"Oh no, please, Ray . . ."

"No, fuck off, right. I'm going do this. Oh yeah! Then I'm going to put you in the girl's bogs, yeah. And I'm going to section it off. Then, I'm going to get every girl down there to leave whoever they're with at the moment and walk in one by one and blow you off while you sit on the bog."

Stevie laughs.

Ray does not join him. "I'm fucking serious, mate!" He fixes Stevie with his large eyes and he shuffles unsteadily, a couple of paces towards him.

Stevie holds his hands out, set to steady the captain's tottering frame. "No, really. You'll only embarrass me if you do that, Ray. I'm not kidding you now." Stevie then observes a cloud of concern draw across the England captain's face. Stevie wheels around and bumps into the tall guy with the limp.

"Cigarette break," Stevie informs the giant. He does not reply. Stevie flicks the rest of the cigarette into the middle of the street.

As they follow the tall guy past the ropes and slowly down the stairs, Stevie is even less convinced of the likelihood of Ray being allowed to accompany Soraya out of those front doors in the next few minutes. At the foot of the stairs, the tall guy turns left to the main dance floor and Ray tugs Stevie's wrists and points in the opposite direction – to the bathroom.

"You stick with me, Stevie," says Ray. They're standing side by side at the urinal. "When's your next tour of duty start?"

"In a couple of months."

"Well, you've got a couple of months' partying to do. The good life. You fucking deserve it."

The tall guy awaits them at the entrance to the main dance floor. He's alongside Soraya. Her face is a picture of pain and panic. They all make their way back to their positions at the table.

Stevie allows Soraya to pour him yet another glass of champagne that he's not going to drink and he glances at his watch. His mind is befuddled enough as it is. She rubs her knees against his and she smiles weakly. He turns his face away and he glimpses through a gap in the crowd someone glowering at him from the bar. He stretches his neck out to get a closer look and to verify his suspicion. It's Bruce and the guy's face is bright orange. Stevie leans even further forward for a closer look, but now his view is blocked by the scores of rhythmically swaying bodies in front of him. He rises to his feet.

Soraya tugs hard at his shirt. He slumps back down into his cushion. "What's up?" he asks her.

"Not feeling well," she replies.

"I'll tell Ray."

"Don't tell him anything," she says. And she's louder than she intended.

"What are you going to do?"

"I want to go home," she says with a childlike pout.

"Without Ray?"

"He won't go unless you're going."

"Don't be ridiculous," Stevie tells her.

"I'm sure. And he needs to go home. He's got training. He's got a qualifying game. He asked me to promise him we wouldn't stay out late. He's got training. Can you tell him you're going? He likes you."

A camera flash. Seconds later a scuffle breaks out at Ray's end of the table. The tall guy has to wrestle down a drunken tourist keen on keeping hold of the sneaky snap he took of Ray. Stevie uses the moment to stand up and glance towards the bar. He can't see Bruce. He turns to Soraya. "I'm going to the bathroom," he tells her.

Stevie checks the smaller room, the main dance floor and the bathroom. There's no sign of Bruce in the club now. Did he really see him earlier or was it a spectral vision conjured up by his champagne-clouded mind? He's standing at the foot of the staircase, wondering what move to make, when Ray approaches, alone.

"Hey, I'm leaving," Stevie tells him.

Ray wags his finger in the air. The movement seems to take place in slow motion, like he's hypnotised himself by the action. Or like he's on slow-motion action replay. "Party's just begun," he drawls. "You ain't even pissed yet, motherfucker."

"I'm starving."

"They can knock us up something here. I can have it arranged. You want something here?"

All wrinkled brows and pursed lips, Stevie feigns to give the suggestion some thought. "I can't eat in this type of place," he says eventually. He's on his way up the stairs.

"Wait! Wait!" Ray calls after him. "You're right. My own stomach's grumbling." He places his hand against his stomach for emphasis. "Wait, man. Please. I've got a spit roast prepared at mine. What'd you say?" He winks at Stevie. "My treat. Let's put the R into R&R."

Stevie fixes him with a long, interrogatory stare. The England captain can hardly stand. He's using the wall as a support. Surely he's too far gone for double entendres. "Let's get Soraya," Stevie ventures.

"I'll go get her," slurs Ray, beginning to turn.

Stevie stops him. "No, I'll get her. You wait here."

Back at the table, the tall guy waves Stevie over. Before he can say anything, Stevie points him to a man wearing a checked sports jacket over a white shirt. "This guy's been asking questions about Ray," he tells him.

"Like what?"

Stevie shakes his head disconsolately. "Just odd stuff."

"Where's Ray?"

Stevie points in the direction of the DJ booth. It takes him half a minute, but as soon as the tall guy starts making his way over there, Stevie yanks Soraya's arm and he rushes her towards the exit. Her towering presence helps detach Ray from the grip of two giggling blondes who had him pinioned to the wall with his red-rimmed eyes staring vacuously into the cameras of their mobile phones. Stevie hangs back, mobile phone in hand, and allows Soraya to push Ray up the stairs to the exit. Stevie keeps an eye out for the tall guy coming up from behind them.

Soraya has her arms around Ray's shoulders now and Stevie is about two steps behind them – too far back to help when a drunken Ray smacks his toe against the last riser and stumbles at the exit and crashes forward, almost taking Soraya face down with him. Stevie rushes forward and helps the security guys to bundle them both into the back of the Lexus. The windows are tinted. Stevie jumps into the front seat and the vehicle speeds off down Air Street.

Stevie's phone goes off. He places it to his ear. It's Bruce.

"You've got to get them back in the club," he barks.

Steve pauses. He cannot believe his ears. "What's up?"

"Is that your missus?" whispers Ray.

"We missed the shot!" shouts Bruce. "His head was down from the jump and then he slipped and fell out the frame. Then two Mercs went by and blocked the shot. All we have is a shot of you and her!"

"OK," says Stevie. He noticed the two cars going by earlier.

"Get them both back in there now!" screams Bruce.

Stevie adjusts his position to shove the phone into his

pocket. "Look, guys," he says to his fellow passengers as they circle the roundabout. "We've got to go back!"

"What's up?" asks Soraya.

"I lost my watch back there," Stevie tells them. It was all he could think of.

"How'd you do that?" groans Soraya.

"Don't ask."

"Hey look, it's on your left arm!" comments the cheeky chauffeur.

"No, I had one on the other arm," protests Stevie blushing in an instant. A huge hand grasps his forearm. He twists in his seat to observe Ray's face between the driver and the front passenger seat. The England captain has removed his gigantic Breitling from his own wrist and is trying gamely to place it around Stevie's.

"No use fighting," grins the chauffeur, glancing briefly at Stevie and then back to the road ahead of him. The chauffeur raises his hand from the gearstick and shoves his Breitling-bearing wrist into Stevie's face. "Ray never takes no for an answer." The chauffeur cackles with laughter and hits down hard on the accelerator. Stevie allows the watch to go over his wrist. He finds it harder to reach into his pocket with that chunky accessory on, but with some effort he manages eventually, and he pulls out his phone again and turns it off.

SPROG

I was raised with Jack, my older brother, in Stratford, East London. The job was single-handedly achieved by my widowed father in between him working nights as a club singer and spending daylight hours sleeping or hunched over the piano, composing musicals that would never see the lights of a stage or reach ears beyond our own and those of his indomitably optimistic agent. When I dropped out of university, I worked in a nursery for a few years and then I moved to Mile End with my boyfriend, who, with some help from the East London Small Business Centre, had started up a computer repair business near the Bow flyover.

My upbringing was high on personal freedom but low on the frequency of common family intimacies. So, even now, nightly "I love you's and emotional outbursts of the kind I see from people playing families on television, look and sound strange and fake to me. When my boyfriend challenges me about this, I joke that it's a consequence of being raised with real blokes. This emotional reserve probably accounted for my discomfort with Jack's needy tone when he called me up one Saturday afternoon and asked that I come down to visit him right away. He'd always been someone I looked up to as the cool, emotionally self-sufficient older brother. So he sounded like another person. As a sentiment, emotional desperation had had as much place in our household as uncooked rice in a cake recipe. I hadn't seen him since last Christmas, when we'd visited Dad for lunch. But I agreed to meet him a hundred metres from the flat he shared with his partner, Diana, near the Queen Victoria pub in Maryland.

According to him, it had started when he walked into the supermarket on the Wednesday of that week. He wasn't sure what he wanted to eat but he was going to see what caught his eye. He'd grabbed a blue, plastic basket from the stacks positioned at the entrance. The supermarket was airy and very cool – in contrast to the stifling heat outside. Goose bumps appeared on his bare arms when only seconds before, those arms had been coated with sweat following his walk from the flat.

Apart from something to eat, he needed dental floss, bin bags and kitchen foil. It seemed like every other day he ended up walking the aisles of Stratford Sainsbury looking for dinner or fillings for Diana's packed-lunch sandwiches.

"It's because you don't form a plan," Diana would say. "Why don't you think about what we need and then do one big shop and not have to worry about it for a while?" she would ask him.

He'd never thought about it. For him, it was just a habit he'd fallen into. One thing was certain. It wasn't for the love of shopping that he ended up there almost every day. As was usual for a Wednesday, he'd timed his visit for 7.15 p.m., knowing that the bow-legged Greek guy would shortly come around marking reduced prices on some of the cooked meats a couple of hours before closing time.

On the cooked meats aisle, he picked up a marked-down beef item. He let it drop into his plastic basket. He'd arrived on the bathroom and toiletries aisle and stood before a row of dental floss when second thoughts about that beef item seeped into his head. He spun around and headed back. He was again on the cooked meats aisle. The bow-legged guy was in deep, whispered conversation with a customer, so he cruised past him and speed-walked to another guy in store uniform lingering at the end of the aisle. He held the package up to the attendant's eye.

"Chinese crispy chilli beef," read the attendant. He then regarded Jack with a questioning expression on his face.

"Now, what I want to know," said Jack, "is whether the beef itself is from China or if the beef's from London and just cooked in the Chinese style."

There'd been news reports less than two days earlier about an outbreak of foot-and-mouth disease. Images of herds of cows lumbering across his television screen had stuck in his head. The story itself had been going for more than a few days now. There'd been some ruckus by a group of Hindu protesters who were pissed off about the cows being killed like that.

"Doesn't it say on the packet?" offered the attendant.

"Nah. It don't say where the beef's from."

The attendant paused as if to gather his thoughts. "It's a bit far to import beef from, ain't it?" he considered. "I mean, all the way from China."

"So, it's English beef?"

He scratched his chin. "I wouldn't want to say, mate."

This was never going to be good enough for Jack. Right then, he made his mind up to get the lamb or the chicken instead. He retraced his steps to the cooked meats aisle. The bow-legged guy was still preoccupied. His pricing gun might have been an item headed for the refuse bin the way it hung limply from his fingers as he continued this private conversation with his friend. He hadn't yet got around to the lamb and chicken items. Jack sighed. It was such sloppy customer service, and as he approached the guy it crossed his mind to shoulder-barge him just enough to shake him out of his torpor. He made a start, but he pulled out at the last second and instead eased past with a sidelong glare.

He hadn't observed such sloppiness at Sainsbury for a long while. And it pained him to be on the receiving end of it. Stratford Sainsbury had been good to us over the years. And it was like watching a loved one being mistreated. For us, in many ways, Stratford Sainsbury had been like a substitute stepmother. On school-day evenings, no sooner would Dad leave for work than out from a rucksack tucked under my bed would spring forth the sponge cakes, glacé cherries, assorted milk chocolates – all pilfered from Stratford Sainsbury that afternoon. That stuff provided respite from the low-sugar and low-fat diet favoured by Dad back then.

This is how we used to work it. Jack would place my empty rucksack in the trolley, and along with the legitimate stuff Dad asked us to buy, we'd include our choices. Jack would then wheel the trolley around till we got to deserted aisles, where he could niftily reach down and sweep the choices into the open rucksack. Jack would then wheel the trolley to the checkout till. I'd lift my rucksack from the trolley in one movement, zip it up and put it over my back. Then we'd pay for the legit stuff and get out of there. A dozy security guard and reliably faulty sensors at the exit allowed us to carry on like this for years. What struck me later was that, no matter how much we tested the seams and stitching of the rucksacks that came and died over the years, we would always head home from the store with an unfulfilled feeling – a feeling not unlike regret. A rucksack could only be so big. It could only carry so much. On the walks home, thoughts of the hundreds of delights still left untried and remaining on those shelves would linger with us. These thoughts would remain even when we got eating, and sometimes for long afterwards.

A few years on, we grew out of these pilfering trips and the Stratford Sainsbury provided our first earned income. Jack started as an aisle assistant, and by the time I joined at sixteen he was already on the tills. Whatever work ethic we possessed was probably instilled courtesy of the then management of Stratford Sainsbury.

Jack dragged his feet to the cake and bread aisle. A fruit bun would go down very nicely with his tea tomorrow afternoon. From the head of the aisle he saw that the bread shelves were in disarray, with brown bread packaging ripped open and stray slices littering the shelves and giving a crazy-paving impression to the floor. His thoughts returned to the sloppy attendant on the cooked meats aisle. The guy would definitely need talking to. He was then distracted, quite suddenly and from an unlikely source. He heard the gurgles first – short and staccato – packets of compressed joy that in total lasted no more than a couple of seconds.

Against the background of silence they came through like bolts of light against a black night sky. His gaze travelled downwards and he found himself face to face with the most delightful-looking, toothless sprog. The sprog gurgled again as if in self-congratulatory acknowledgement of having successfully pulled off the trick of getting his attention. Toothless sprog. In spite of himself, Jack smiled back. Then he looked more closely at the cherub's face. It was strangely compelling. Though the sound was of joy, the eyes held a mischief, an incongruous knowingness. In the brown depths he saw something that had no place in a body of that size. Jack quickly averted his gaze. In your local supermarket, you don't want to get a reputation for staring at kids.

His eyes travelled up from the sprog's face to the woman who stood two paces ahead of the trolley. She had her back to the trolley and she stared intently at the label of a loaf of bread. When she tilted her head, he caught a closer look at her profile. It was a face he knew. He gulped and backed off. It took him a moment to compose himself. He stole another glance at her. Within seconds, the face of the woman's partner came into view and he, too, began staring at the loaf. In low tones, they exchanged words in what Jack figured was Polish. She placed the loaf in her trolley and made to move on with her man in tow.

He wanted to get out of their sight – and quickly. So he retraced his footsteps to the cooked meats section. This was one place where he knew he would be safe from Magda's gaze. He recalled how on their second date they'd gone to an ice-skating rink in Streatham. The activities of the afternoon raised a hunger in them and Jack didn't think he could make the journey back to Stratford without first having something to eat. They were less than fifty metres from the entrance to the Kentucky Fried Chicken when she pulled her hand away from his grip.

"Where we are going?" she asked.

"To the dark side of the moon," he replied. "Where do you think? To get something to eat."

"In there?"

"Yeah."

"No way."

After much cajoling, he managed to get her through the doors and seated at a table. Emboldened by this success, he asked her to join him with his Deluxe Boneless Box.

"Do they cook anything else here?" she scowled.

"Why won't you have the chicken?" he insisted.

"You know why."

He fixed her with a serious stare. "What are you going to have? A coleslaw? Vegetables are no less living things than the chicken was," he told her.

"Forget it."

In mock exasperation, he kept shaking his head exaggeratedly as he munched on. "Any way you choose to look at it, Magda, whether you eat an animal or a vegetable, it's life being ripped apart."

"I'll have some fruit, Jack. If they serve fruit here."

He laughed. But he returned to the issue after he'd taken a few bites of his chicken. "Fruits are living and feeling things," he told her, in the manner of a teacher talking to a kid.

She nodded. "But if you take a fruit from a tree," she responded, "that fruit gets replaced by another leaf or fruit. It's not a death."

"It's the death of that fruit."

"You are what you eat," she sighed, and turned to stare out of the window. "Do you have this expression here?" Then she turned her eyes to his plate. "Do you know that in Africa the warriors eat the heart of the lion to make them brave?"

"They don't serve lion meat in Western Europe, babe."

"But Jack, what do you think you'll be if you eat animals farmed like this chicken here – animals farmed one on top of another so they spend their whole life not moving?"

"Fruits and vegetables don't move."

"They're not supposed to move."

Her reason for not sleeping with him that night had nothing to do with the banal retort of not knowing him well enough yet, but rather on account of him so recently having consumed a mass produced animal.

"So, shall I hang around till I digest it a bit more?"

"But you'll still have quarter of the poor beast stuck between your teeth!"

No. Magda would never find herself on the cooked meats aisle of a supermarket.

It had been three years since she said she was leaving East London. Jack wondered whether she'd returned to live here with her new man. Years later, I would still wonder whether he would have felt less strongly if he'd recognised her first and then saw the baby, or whether it was the fact that the baby made an impression first that had got him so shaken.

They'd first met when Jack was working at the H&M store on the corner of Oxford Street and Regent Street.

The management had just started trialling a scheme to have a DJ spin tunes in the store on Saturdays. It was his second week on the job when Magda had come in wearing a white taffeta mini-dress and gold-coloured, gladiator-style sandals not unlike those she was wearing in the supermarket. He'd sneaked away from his post. He felt compelled to talk to her. He'd already tapped her on the shoulder before he'd formed the words he wanted to say. When she'd turned, all he could do was smile stupidly. He'd asked for her mobile number and she'd refused. He'd asked her whether she worked nearby and she'd told him that she was a nanny in Godalming and was trying to pick up something in the sales because her boss was having a dinner party later that evening. Then he told her his name and asked for hers. She seemed friendly enough. He was about to try for her number again when the manager began making his way back to the store entrance. Jack retreated to his station, thinking to catch Magda on her way out. But she didn't remain long in the store. The manager was still lingering around the decks when she began making her way out. Jack's eyes followed her as she passed through the open exit doors and then disappeared into the teeming crowds on Oxford Street.

That might have been the last he saw of her, had they not bumped into each other quite by accident two weeks later. It happened in Gants Hill. She was at the bus stop on her way to Woodford, where her friend lived. She was being harassed by a teenager in a baseball cap when Jack had walked up and sat himself on the plastic seat next to her. She turned and recognised him right away. She grinned. He told her it was fate. She said he was corny.

He asked for her number. This time she said yes. Later that very night, they went out for the first time.

If you drew a line graph charting the joy factor in their relationship over the year they were together, it would look as spiky as the business end of a tooth-saw blade. But my boyfriend would say graphs are a crap choice of tool to display anything remotely relating to feelings. We met Magda just once, when she'd chosen to come with Jack to our flat. Even if she hadn't been the first foreign-born girl I'd seen Jack with, she would have been memorable to me. Back then, she wore her hair long, just touching her shoulders, and she wore very little make-up save for a touch of lipstick. Though she must have been about twenty at the time, I didn't regard her with the muted sigh of pity I would give to the Debbies, Rosies and Kims he'd sometimes introduce me to over the years. Even then, I sensed a strength about her that put her in a different league to the other girls. Not that she said anything much. It was all in the way she carried herself.

She accompanied Jack when, on the umpteenth time of asking, he turned up to fix a leak from our shower pump. We'd hoped they'd stay for lunch. But she'd already booked them on the Chelsea Walk. This tour took in Sloane Square tube station, the King's Road, Danvers Street and Cheyne Walk. Then the group would return to Sloane Square tube station. She was always finding somewhere interesting to visit on a weekend. Jack had never seen as much of the city he was born and raised in as during his run with Magda.

He'd been out on a drinking session the night before and he was grateful when finally they arrived at St Luke's church and the guide suggested the group pause for a break. Jack loosened the laces of his trainers and thought he heard his stifled feet purr with gratitude. The others pulled packed lunches from their bags as the plummy tones of the portly tour guide were replaced by foreign accents, laughter and high-pitched shrieks from the younger members of the group seeking release, having been reined in by silence for the past thirty minutes. Jack took the opportunity to relax and, leaning his back against a low stone wall, he closed his eyes for a while. Magda wandered away and once or twice when he opened his eyes he caught sight of her smoking and chatting animatedly to the tour guide. The guide's booming laughter would put an end to any chance of his drifting into sleep.

But then, quite suddenly, it seemed she was standing above him, tugging at his hands and asking that they leave right away.

"I don't get it," he told her. "We're just over halfway there."

"It's not going to be good any more!" she declared and she was already striding away.

His assumption was that she'd finally given in to the tiredness she'd been heroically beating back with the energy drinks she'd packed into her bag. He'd joined her the previous night for a farewell do for one of her language school classmates that had turned into a six-hour bender. Although she hadn't drunk half as much as he had, she'd put some away. Back home on his sofa later that afternoon, she collapsed her face against his shoulder.

"I've been working for six months," she said vacantly. Then she repeated the phrase with a slight variation. "I've been working here for six months." She paused. "What's wrong with that?"

"Nothing," he said.

"I thought it was correct sentence."

"It's a perfectly good sentence," he told her. "Short and to the point."

"Yeah," she pouted. "It was all I needed to say for someone to know I was a foreigner."

In six months, Magda had progressed from no English at all to the point where she had as good a command of the language as many native people Jack knew. Her rapid progress had much to do with the way she had learned the language. A lot of mimicry was involved, a bit like how a child learns a language. The worst question anyone could ask within minutes of striking up a conversation with her was where she was from. To make her feel better, Jack muttered something about the slightest inflection being detectable to the English ear.

"English ear!" she cried. "He was a French guy!"

"I thought it was the tour guide you were talking about."

"No, didn't you see the little guy with the black and red Nike rucksack who came up to us when – ?"

"I hadn't noticed him."

"You're the least observant guy ever."

"I won't argue with that," he conceded.

The following Sunday she booked them both on a River Thames cruise. The wisecracking tour guide had completed his welcomes and introduction and the boat had just set off when quite suddenly she turned to him.

"Of all the English actresses you know . . . " she began.

"I don't know any actresses," he quipped.

"Seen on TV or wherever," she countered irritably. "Who do you think sounds the best?"

"Who do I think sounds the best?" Jack repeated, buying himself seconds of reflection time. It wasn't something he'd given any thought to. But he sensed that she wanted a quick response.

"Joanna Lumley," he said. It was a name that had just sprung into his head.

"Never heard of this one," she said.

"Good voice," he assured her.

Within half an hour of docking back on Embankment Pier, she was dragging him down the aisles of Waterstone's bookshop on Charing Cross Road. She strolled out with an audio copy of *Esio Trot and the Minpins* under her arm and the sounds from that disc never left her ears for the following weeks until her manner of speaking had been completely altered. Now Jack had nothing against Joanna Lumley tones – provided they came from the mouth of Joanna Lumley. But over the following months, Magda's insistence on talking that way all the time made him feel like every emotion she expressed was fake or at least contrived. This put a strain on the relationship.

The golden period of their run together began as a consequence of another throwaway line. As they'd walked out of a movie one early afternoon, she'd asked him, about when he was born.

"But you know my date of birth," he reminded her.

She smiled broadly, her parted lips exposing the purple tongue given her by the blackcurrant drinks she'd been sipping throughout the movie. "No, I mean exactly when – like the hour and minute of the day you were born."

"I don't know," he confessed.

"Well, find out," she urged him, and she ran off to collect the kids from school.

Her tone had been playful but she didn't let it go. On every subsequent meeting she would ask for that time of birth, and when with a regretful sigh he'd begin to confess how once again he'd forgotten to check, she'd cut him short with a dig in the ribs and threaten to leave right away. Eventually he interrupted Dad on a composing session and got a birth time to the nearest hour. He heard nothing more about the issue for a few weeks until one Saturday she came by his room carrying a thin booklet, which she opened on her lap. On the opened page, a huge circle intersected with broken lines and mysterious glyphs meant, according to her wildly enthusiastic commentary, that they were soulmates who had been destined to meet.

"But I told you that ages ago," he reminded her.

She slapped him on the thigh. "I'm serious," she protested. "You just wait and see!" Then, in a more confidential tone, she told him, "You know, for two people, the most important thing is that they keep moving. And that they want to move in the same direction. If they're not moving in the same direction, no matter how much they like each other, it's not going to work for them. Now I know we can move in the right direction."

That August, the family she worked for left their Surrey home for a two-week holiday in the Maldives. Jack invited himself around, hoping she'd want the company. He was also keen to avoid home visits from his landlord, to whom he owed three months' rent. They spent the first few days relaxing by day and by night, depleting their hosts' wine cellar and murdering the springs of their three-seater sofa.

It was during this period that she attempted, unwittingly perhaps, to recruit him to the ranks of Smiths and Morrissey devotees. He'd left himself open to the move, having failed to bring around any of his own CDs. They would lie on the patio as the sun beat down on their exposed flesh. She would tap her feet and sing along to these albums, sometimes taking the melody, sometimes sharing a harmony with her hero and rising from her sun lounger only to change CDs or to refill her cocktail glass. Jack had this aversion to Morrissey. He mistrusted wordy songs. For him, music was to dance to. If he wanted social or philosophical insight, he'd go to a library shelf. He didn't need that stuff from pop singers. He also had his fears about her love of the Smiths. The group was not of their generation. He suspected the influence of an older lover – perhaps a first love, whose memory she was swooning to right now as she lay on that sun lounger with her eyes closed and her innermost thoughts locked away from him beneath a serene and distant expression.

One Thursday evening, she announced that the next day she'd be going to the clinic for a smear. They'd moved the TV from the living room to the bedroom for the night. Their favourite sheets were in the washing machine and so they lay side by side on the bare mattress. They'd just watched a documentary about music moguls. Jack let her know right away that he would not be walking into that clinic. He had a fear of hospitals that was matched only by my own fear of rodents. He said he would wait for her outside or that he would wait there in the house till she came back. She shrugged. She was easy-going about such things and didn't seem to mind.

"But what would you prefer to do?" she added after a moment.

"How do you mean?"

"Would you prefer to wait outside the clinic or wait here?"

"I'll wait outside the clinic," he said.

She didn't seem to mind that choice, either. Her expression was a replica of the one of relaxed contentment bordering on ennui that she'd been wearing for most of the day. But moments later, she asked him a question.

"Haven't you got anything else to be doing?" she asked him. She registered his unease. But she didn't change tack. "You've been here for about a week now," she observed.

"That's right. And what of it?"

"I'm just surprised you haven't anything else to do."

He tilted his head back and laughed. "Calling me a layabout now?"

"You do seem more relaxed than most guys I've been out with."

Perhaps he'd been kidding himself that he'd grown accustomed to it. But, for the first time in the week, her Joanna Lumley tones began to mildly irritate him. With his eyes still fixed on the television, Jack reached for the cigarette packet on the dresser. It felt despairingly light in his palm. He flicked it open and had his suspicion confirmed when he frowned down on a solitary cigarette left in there. She was still speaking when he told her he was off to the twenty-four-hour petrol station to get more supplies.

"Do you want anything besides fags?"

She shook her head.

He pulled a pair of tracksuit bottoms over his shorts. Outside, a light wind played with the baggy sleeves of the polo shirt he'd been wearing. As he approached a Baby Bentley, one of the top-of-the-range vehicles that lined the road, a solitary ginger cat scurried underneath it. Within sight of the petrol station kiosk, he phoned to ask if she was sure she didn't want some ice cream. The freezer had suddenly stopped working and he wasn't about to open a whole tub if she couldn't share some of it at least. Her mobile rang a few times. It was probably still downstairs in the garden. He gave up. At the kiosk he called out for just a packet of Marlboros. He smoked the first one as he sat on the short perimeter wall of the forecourt. A feeling of peace descended on him as, eyes to the road, with his legs stretched out in front of him, the nicotine began to do its work. The night-time traffic was light.

A voice broke the silence. He turned. A young woman was seated in the passenger seat of a red convertible parked outside one of the pumps. The top was down and she spoke again. She wanted to know what time it was. The car was an Audi. Jack couldn't imagine that a car with Audi specifications would be wanting for a clock on its dashboard. The girl was blonde and tanned, in her early twenties, he guessed. Her tone was playful, her expression . . . flirtatious. She glanced back at her friend – a tall redhead who was still buying something at the kiosk. Jack checked the clock on his mobile and to his own astonishment saw that it was 3.30 a.m. He let her know. She smiled a lazy smile and Jack felt himself being aroused by the manner of this girl. He'd never been sexually faithful to any of his partners, so he felt less guilty than surprised by his impulses. Because, if someone had asked him fifteen minutes earlier, he'd have put his level of horniness at zero. He'd left Magda only minutes before and now, here he was, aroused by a woman not half as attractive – a woman outside the range of types he normally considered attractive, and a woman he'd seen from waist up only . . . a woman who had simply asked him for the time. When her red-haired friend returned to the car, he heard them exchange some words and then, with a wolf whistle, they sped off into the night, leaving him with the feeling that he'd been rescued from himself.

His thoughts turned to the intimate side of his relationship with Magda. He'd been so looking forward to spending this week with her. Their sex sessions had always been sporadic. But the first three days here had been wild. It was the first time they'd enjoyed such an uninterrupted period of time together. And it was as if he'd been trying to make up for intimate moments lost to conflicting moods, views and schedules during the greater part of their run together. But for the past three days they might as well have been adolescent brother and sister for the lack of physical intimacy. Further, he had a feeling that very soon they'd start getting on each other's nerves. They'd already begun firing cheap shots; a sure sign, he'd come to recognise, of a descent into one of their realms of competitive displays of surliness. He knew they needed to have a conversation.

Back at the front door, he felt his pockets. He hadn't taken her keys with him. He rang the bell and waited for her footsteps to come down the stairs. He'd known the weather was weird lately, so he'd been rash to sprint out without a jumper. It was only now that he was really feeling the chill. He rang the bell again and waited. Still no answer. The light was on in the bedroom. He tossed a small stone up at the window and called out softly to her. He couldn't shout too loudly. If neighbours poked their heads through their open windows, none would recognise him. The first thing they'd do would be to call the police. Twenty minutes later, he was still standing outside her door. He'd left his finger on the front doorbell so that it rang continuously.

Thankfully, his wallet was with him. And there, within its compartments, nestled his door key. There was no money left in the wallet, though. It would be asking for trouble to remain standing there. He began the long walk home.

He telephoned her the next day. He got no response. He left a text message and that went unresponded to as well. A week later, without warning, she turned up on his doorstep bearing a chocolate cake. She made no mention of her no-show. But it was never the same after that week at her place, and the relationship petered out. One morning, he walked down the stairs and on his way to the kitchen saw a single letter lying on the doormat. The envelope bore her handwriting. He opened it. She'd secured a job as part of a sales team in central London and would be moving house to rent a room of her own in Ealing. By then, he'd already begun seeing someone else.

I got to the Queen Victoria late. I met Jack standing outside. He held a pint glass in his hand. It was half-full. He had flattened out a tabloid newspaper against the window ledge and I did not recognise him instantly.

The new haircut was severe and it made him look much older than he did when I saw him at Christmas. I told him so and he admitted as much in an instant. But he shrugged as if he hardly cared. *I'm a man in a crisis and barely holding myself together* was so deeply etched across his unshaven face, that I reckoned on stepping out, the impression his physical appearance would make on his younger sister had held as much interest for him as the weekend weather forecast for Borneo.

"Shall we go in?" I asked him.

He shook his head and stepped across to block my path. "Someone's just come in," he told me. "That's why I'm here."

"You must have fucked half your neighbourhood by now," I said to him through gritted teeth. "Perhaps it really is time to move on. You can't hide from your neighbours for ever, can you?"

"It's not like that," he replied and he gulped the remains of his pint. "Let's head off down the road."

We moved to King Edward VII pub, where I ordered two more pints. Once we'd sat down he didn't need much prompting to get to the business at hand. The encounter at the supermarket was on his mind. "She was twenty and attractive when you first met her," I told him. "Should be no surprise that years on, she would find someone to start a family with. It's a law of life that people will move on." I'd already decided that what he didn't need was soft words and sympathy. Besides, coming from me, that kind of talk would only have sounded strange to his ears.

He nodded. "It's not so simple."

"What did the guy look like?"

"Kinda cool. Of course, I don't have much to go on. A lot of this is instinctive. But actually he seemed the kind of guy I would like." He reflected. "And not many guys I can say that about."

"Does that make it harder for you?" I asked.

"I'm not sure."

"Did she see you?"

"I doubt it."

"She probably wouldn't have recognised you, if she did."

He sighed and took a long gulp of his beer. Face-to-face it was too sadly apparent how shaken he'd been by all this. He confessed that he hadn't had two hours' continuous sleep since the chance sighting of that infernal sprog.

"I'm no psychologist," I told him, "but, though you're no spring chicken, I would have thought you're still too young for regret to do this to you."

"It's not that simple," he said. He raised his eyes to me. "It was the kid."

"What about it?"

He rubbed his face. "It said something to me."

"Said something to you?"

"Yeah, by the time I got to the checkout I'd got Magda to the back of my mind, and I was concentrating on getting my stuff into the bags when they passed by me on their way out . . ."

"And the kid said something to you?"

He nodded.

"Jack, on the phone you said the kid was a baby – no teeth, even."

"I know."

"You're tripping."

"At what age do they start talking?" he wanted to know.

"You should have had first-hand knowledge by now."

"Skip it."

"Well, quite a while after they get some teeth, let me tell you. And it's a good while after that before they can convey thought."

"Fuck that." He was shaking his head.

"So the baby said something to you. You sure it wasn't Magda you heard?"

"Magda was speaking in Polish."

"The kid said something to you in English?"

"The kid said something to me in English."

"What, something funny? Something nasty? Something nice?"

"It wasn't nice."

"What'd the kid say?"

He regarded me with sad eyes that told me the words had been torturing his mind for close on a week. "I can't tell you," he said. There was such a note of finality to his tone when he said this. I decided not to press.

His pint glass was now empty and I noticed his glance to check the level of mine. I remembered I'd been to this pub before, as a student, when it used to host quiz nights. Today most of the clientele consisted of guys discussing sport. I asked him if he wanted another pint. He shook his head.

"Let's go to the supermarket," he offered.

"Stratford Sainsbury?"

He shrugged. "Why not?"

I studied his face for a moment. "What do you expect to gain from that?"

He remained silent.

"It's unlikely she's moved back here, Jack. She could have been shopping for a friend nearby, or anything."

"Coming?"

I ended up trailing him as he trawled the aisles for close to half an hour seeking lord knows what from the face of that speaking sprog. When he called the following week with the same request, I cried off on account of a doctor's appointment. When he called two days later, I did the same. Then he stopped calling.

I received a letter from Diana a couple of months later. It was very brief. She asked whether I'd seen Jack lately. She'd left for work and come back to find his case missing, along with all his books. He'd left his CD and DVD collection. He'd also left his mobile phone. But he hadn't even left a note.

I phoned Dad immediately. He'd received an email from Jack a week before. Much of what he'd written was random reminiscences. But he had also written about spending time in Dorset. He hadn't said whether it was for work or simply for a holiday.

Then he'd made a reverse charge call from a Dorset payphone. Over the phone, Dad had played him the opening scene of a show he was composing and had great hopes for. All the while, Dad had assumed that Jack had left for Dorset with Diana. Now he was suggesting I pop over and speak to Diana when I had time over the weekend.

"She may need the company now," he said.

ADULT EDUCATION

When she hears the thuds on the stairs, Sabrina places the pharaonic head carefully back on the mantelpiece. It's not an expensive ornament, but ten times she's asked Lindsay to sell it to her and ten times Lindsay has refused. The living room door opens and Lindsay walks in with her handbag sandwiched under her left arm and dragging two wheeled suitcases behind her. Sabrina watches her in silence as she leaves the cases in the middle of the room and steps over to the wine rack in the corner. Lindsay is wearing red, high-heeled shoes and a short red dress.

"How long have you been living here?" Sabrina asks her.

"Five years. Thereabouts. Why?"

"Something not quite right about this place."

"How'd you mean?"

"It's off-key, man."

Lindsay pauses to consider. "Off-key, man? What does that expression mean? Off-key, man. Can you leave your ghetto talk for East London?"

"It's spooky," Sabrina tells her. "It's a spooky place. Gives me the creeps."

"You've been coming here for six weeks and you choose this moment to let me know that?"

"It's a good time. You're leaving."

"Yeah, leaving for a while! I have to come back, remember." Lindsay examines the label of a wine bottle. It's the third one she's opened in a couple of hours. "Have you seen things?" she asks distractedly.

"No," Sabrina replies. "Haven't seen anything. At least not yet. Heard things, though."

"Pah. I'd be more concerned if you hadn't heard things. Houses on this street are hundreds of years old. The floorboards still carry the weight of thousands of souls gone by. This place has its own character – which is more than I can say about the new-build monstrosities where I expect you saw the light of day."

Sabrina watches her tackle a bottle with a corkscrew. "You know what?" she says. "I don't mean to be rude, but I really need to get out of here."

"Well, you know I'm with you on that." Lindsay pauses in her efforts. "I don't want to be awkward, but that money I owe you . . . Would you take a cheque instead?"

"A cheque? No."

"I was planning to use up these notes on the taxi to the airport and for our night out tonight."

"Our night? I told you, I'm not going."

"Sabrina, I insist you do."

"Told you I'm not."

"So you won't take a cheque?"

"I can't take a cheque. I'm putting nothing into that bank account at the moment. It's dead."

Lindsay emits a theatrical sigh and sets the wine bottle

down on the coffee table. "Well, I guess a university student without a bank account isn't a completely novel situation." She begins counting out some notes then stops herself. "Look, Sabrina," she says. "I know it's none of my business, but I guess on your very last day I'm allowed to ask why you do this."

"Do what?"

"This job. I mean you come here twice a week and you really put in the work, I'd say."

"For love."

"Because it's not a short distance you come," Lindsay observes, ignoring the quip. "And you do put in some effort."

She hands the notes over to Sabrina.

"You think so?"

"I'd say."

"Well, thank you, Lindsay. I didn't think you'd appreciate it that much. Me and Cyrus are saving."

"You and Cyrus are saving. OK." She paused. "Boob job? White van? Pet crocodile?"

"Can't say."

"Course you can."

Sabrina stares past her.

"No?"

"No."

"I reckon you're saving for a deposit on a flat to rent," says Lindsay, after opening the bottle and pouring out a couple of drinks.

"If you say so."

"Outgrown the nest, is it? How old did you say you were?"

"I've never told you my age."

"Nineteen, give or take a year?"

"Close enough."

"Right, Sabrina. This is all very interesting. But, as I said, I really do want you to join me tonight."

"You should be staying in and getting some rest. You've got a long flight tomorrow."

"That's right. With plenty of time to sleep on the plane. Look, Sabrina, I intend for you to get into that taxi with me and make a night out of this. I've already booked a hotel next to the airport."

"I mean, if I could go . . . I would."

"But you can come."

"Told you. I've committed – "

"You saw Cyrus yesterday and the day before and the day before. You'll no doubt meet him tomorrow and the day after that, and perhaps the day after that one. He'll take you to the local cinema, the local takeaway or the local pub – same as he's done a hundred times before. Right now, I can take you somewhere you've never been."

Sabrina smiles politely as she accepts a glass of red wine. "But we arranged for today," she sighs. "That's the point."

Lindsay slumps on to the sofa. "Hmm. You know, I don't look a candidate to be giving anyone life lessons."

"But you're going to give me some anyway right?"

"Thirty-five years old. Three ex-husbands in six years; childless; a tendency to drink more than any sensible person should – take more risks than any sensible person should. But one thing I do know – one thing I've found . . ."

"OK, here it comes."

". . . is that, while constancy to causes may be a good thing, sometimes – just sometimes – constancy to individuals, especially young guys, seldom leads further than the bottom of a JD bottle. That's all I'm going to say."

"And that's been your experience, right?"

"It depends where you are. Impetuousness in a five-year-old can come across as cute. In a thirty-five-year-old it's downright folly. For a teenager like yourself . . ."

"I haven't told you my age, Lindsay."

". . . to be dedicated to anything but your own self-discovery and discovery of the world, isn't a good bet. I know this counselling-type talk may not become me . . ."

"You're not wrong,"

". . . but this time, this is the time of your life . . ." She breaks off, then resumes just as suddenly. "Sabrina, you'll never look as good as you do right now. You'll never feel as well . . . And you should . . . It's just a concern to me, Sabrina. And I've listened to the way you talk. I notice things. It's just a concern to me that, at your age, how little you use the first person singular when talking about your day-to-day life and plans."

"You what?"

"You very well know what I mean. All this 'we . . .' 'we . . .' 'we . . .' 'me and Cyrus', 'Cyrus and I'. What's that about?"

"You tell me."

"Don't think about asking me to explain why. But I just feel I shouldn't be here tonight. I'll go out with you or without you. Preferably with you."

"Nope."

"No?"

"No."

"OK."

"What, are you lonely or something?"

"I'm alone. Never lonely."

"That old one, eh? I mean, you've got all this money and this place is furnished like a seminary. Just look at it. Why don't you get a telly or something – like everyone else?"

"A television? Oh, it's a cowardly way of being entertained."

"I tell you what – your marriages might have lasted longer if you had. Would have stopped you nagging them to the door."

"Ouch!"

"Sorry."

"That's OK. I see you've got me down as shallow."

"I never said that."

"My mother would say that most people are irredeemably shallow. They lack the inner resources to maintain long-term relationships. And that, when you hear of a long, successful marriage, you can guarantee one thing." She grabs Sabrina's mobile phone from the table. "You can bet your life it's between people who've managed to find a way to distance themselves from each other – television, children, and jobs abroad with long periods of separation."

She holds the phone and regards it closely.

"What're you doing?" Sabrina asks when she sees her fingers going to work. Lindsay, she suspects, is scrolling down her contacts list.

"If it's courage you're lacking and you can't find it in you to simply call him, I'm going to phone him and I'm going to tell him that you can't make it because, for a change, you're doing something interesting with your friend, employer and mentor."

Sabrina snatches at the phone but Lindsay is not as drunk as she'd thought. Lindsay pulls niftily away and Sabrina's fingers clutch at thin air. Sabrina stumbles, and from her position on the floor she watches Lindsay hit the dial button and then raise the phone to the side of her head. Sabrina rises and makes a lunge at her and this time she gets a grip on Lindsay's right wrist. Lindsay digs her elbow into Sabrina's side and manages to keep the phone to her ear. With her other hand, Sabrina grabs Lindsay's hair and has a few sharp tugs.

"Christ! You're breaking my wrist!" Lindsay shrieks.

"Well, let go, then!"

Suddenly, Lindsay releases the phone, letting it fall to the floor. The struggle took a lot out of Lindsay. She pants like she's just passed the post on a half-marathon.

"You punched me. You fucking juvenile delinquent."

"You deserved it, you fucking old degenerate."

Lindsay grimaces. "Christ, you've broken my wrist. And you've messed up my hair! I came in looking like a movie star and you've turned me into a scarecrow, you little bitch."

"Good. Maybe now you'll stay in and relax your old bones like you ought to."

Lindsay smoothes down her dress. "You don't only dress like a man, you fight like one, too." She glances down at lower body. "Oh, this isn't good," she judges. After a moment, she staggers to the wine rack again. "Hey, how've you got lover boy saved on your phone, anyway?" she asks over her shoulder.

"How've I got him down? I've got him down as Lado."

"Lado?"

"Long story."

"So, I take it you're definitely not coming with me, then."

"No."

"Even on your very last day in my employ?"

"No."

"Very, very last day?"

"I said no."

"Very, very, very last day? Is there not an ounce of sentiment in that muscle-laden frame of yours?"

"Fuck off."

Lindsay gives up on the selection in the wine rack and heads to the kitchen. She returns with a bottle of vodka in one hand and a full glass in the other. She slumps on to the sofa and, with her free hand, she opens up her handbag.

"Sabrina?"

Lindsay places her glass down and holds up a wodge of notes in the manner of someone teasing a dog with a bone.

Sabrina laughs despite herself. "There's not enough paper in the world you could offer for me to even think about cancelling my date with my Cyrus."

"What if I threw in the pharaonic head? You know you want it. Yours to take away. All you've got to do is the right thing."

"Not happening."

Lindsay stares at her employee as if seeing her for the first time. "Who is this guy Cyrus, anyway?" she asks. "Royalty or something?"

"What's that got to do with anything? I've known him for ten years. I've known you six weeks."

"Well, what's time got to do with it?"

"He's going to be buzzing tonight. He means to cheer me up."

"I didn't suspect you needed cheering up."

"We were having a rough patch. Anyway, he's just had his first proper studio session so his mind will be going a hundred miles an hour when he gets here from the West End."

"Studio session? You didn't tell me he was a nude model."

"He sings."

"We all have our ways of getting through our work, love."

"No, he's been in a recording studio, you div. He's put together a mix tape."

"How very nice."

"Five songs. All of them he's written himself. It's taken almost a year for him to put it together."

"So, he's got a great voice, right?"

"I haven't heard it yet. He's never lets me hear it. It's just music – beats, mainly. Deep down he's shy, really."

"What's he look like, then?"

"What's he look like? Well, how can I put it in words? I just like him. In every way. And he's manly, you know – very physical."

"Very physical," Lindsay repeats to herself. "What does that mean? Does it just mean you like it rough?"

"No, if you listen to me. It's about how he expresses himself."

"Yeah, right. A mindless thug, you mean. All cock and ego."

"He's the most intelligent person I know."

"There's a joke there. But just this once, I'm going to show some restraint. I'm sure you told me once he was the violent type."

"Did I, Lindsay?"

"So, is he violent with you? Is him being physical just black talk for him smacking you around once in a while?"

"I think I told you that he was passionate."

"OK, well, has he ever been 'passionate' with you – outside the bedroom?"

"You know what? No. But I've seen him handle people who've been rude to me," she observes. "Also, it's the way he moves."

"OK. So it's the way he moves now."

"Among other things."

"So, how does he move?" asks Lindsay. Then softly, with a derisive snort to herself, "The way he moves. I've never heard that as a selling factor on a bloke."

Sabrina raises her eyes as if considering. "I can't explain . . . It's like . . . he moves with purpose, you know? Even when he might not be doing or going anywhere special. I can't explain."

"Demonstrate, then. Show me how 'Mr So Wonderful He Can't Be Put On Pause' walks. Just for two minutes, along here. Go on."

"What?"

"Just across here."

"What, here?"

"Yeah, I want to see."

Sabrina considers there is a childlike quality about Lindsay's insistence. Of course, she's drunk out of her mind. "How does he go?" she begins. "He kind of keeps his head down and his arms . . ." Then she stops. "I'm not showing you!"

"Sure you can."

"I can't do it. But he's just got all the things I look for. And I'm not too young to know how hard that is to find. So, just that would have made him an unforgettable person to me. Even if we were only kids when we first met. Anyway, that's the physical part of things. But it's not just that. It's not the main thing."

Lindsay has stopped paying attention. "Sorry to interrupt the eulogy," she says. "But at what age did you start fucking?"

"Pardon me?"

"What age?"

"Did I start fucking, or did I start fucking Cyrus specifically?"

"Did you start fucking 'Mr So Wonderful He Can't Be Put On Pause'?"

"Later than you'd think."

"I've got no moral agenda. Just want to find out for how long you've been at it. Just curiosity."

"We were sixteen."

"Still exciting?"

Sabrina nods affirmatively.

"For you, at least."

"For both of us."

"Well, it's an easy one for us to get suckered on, isn't it? They always come, so I guess we think we always make them happy. But it doesn't always work that way, does it? It's physiological, isn't it? Just the way they're made."

"I'm not following you, Lindsay. Not sure I even want to."

"Your first love?"

"Nope."

"No? How stupid of me. Forgot I was before a representative of the forever-spread-legged generation."

Sabrina laughs. "Course he was. Told you I've known him ten years. But the thing is, our moods and feelings are always in sync. I know people who live together for a while can get that feeling. But that's partly because they wake up together, eat together, can feel tired at the same time, hungry at the same time, moody at the same time. But we've always had that and we've lived separately all the time we've been together. I mean, my friends tell me, and I believe, you can still get that feeling of aloneness when you're with someone. Even if you're doing something together, you know they're experiencing the same thing to a different intensity than you are."

"Get a grip, girl!"

"I'm sure you'd know what I mean if you were sober. For example, one partner suggests, and the other agrees, to go to a firework display together. And just by suspecting the other isn't feeling it as much as you, it spoils the experience for you? Or if you feel the other is compromising a bit. Or if you're compromising, too. It takes away from the feeling of being together. Lindsay, you know what? You won't find a person in the world whose tolerance for anything sub-par in their life is below mine. So the fact I've been with Cyrus for this long shows he must have something – at least, for me."

"Very moving. So you've known him for ten years?"

"Ten years."

"I bet within ten minutes of meeting him I can have his pants around his ankles, his nuts in my hand, his head back, eyes rolling wildly in their sockets."

"Fuck you."

"And him howling down the ceiling like a werewolf."

"Fuck you."

"I'm not trying to aggravate you, Sabrina. It's simply something I'm sure I can do. So, I'm just telling you – that's all."

"Well, thanks for speaking your mind. But fuck you."

"Oh, if you'd just put it to the test, dear girl. I'd send him back to you the worse for wear." Lindsay laughs almost hysterically and for long, as if she was holding up the conjured image for continued contemplation.

"You started drinking too early. I'd better go." Sabrina rises to her feet.

"Yep. Best to run perhaps."

Sabrina checks her phone and lets it fall into her leather tote bag. She moves slowly to the door. "You seriously think you can get my Cyrus to go for you?" she asks, with a teasing lilt in her voice and casually turning to Lindsay.

Lindsay gives her a fixed stare. "That's clear."

"What's clearer is you've been on the sauce too long."

"My head's fine."

"Well, if you think it is, that makes it that much worse." Sabrina sighs. "Oh, my days," she laments, pausing at the door. "You know, apart from earning some dough, I had some expectations when I answered that ad of yours."

"You did?"

"I did. You know – single, university-educated woman, mid-thirties, well travelled . . . And then I met you and you were well-spoken, witty . . ."

"What did you expect to gain?"

"You know, I thought, *This is someone I might be able to learn something from*. This was someone I'd want to be like some day. Maybe I wasn't exactly expecting it but I thought it was a possibility."

"You can still. You can still learn something from me. If you allow yourself to."

"Not what you're offering. You're more filthy than any of the girls I know. Any of the girls I've ever met."

"Come on."

"No, it's true. You're so coarse, Lindsay. And that's saying something, because I grew up in care! Or maybe things just sound coarser to me when it comes from someone like you."

"And why is that?"

"They just do."

"Maybe it's something in you," says Lindsay, and then she belches loudly.

"How'd you mean?"

"It could be a reaction."

"To what?"

"Your outlook . . . Your happiness, I suppose."

"What about it?"

"It provokes me."

Sabrina regards her with suspicion.

"And no, it's not because I'm a jealous old hag. It's just that it rests on such . . . insecure foundations."

"My happiness?"

"Yep."

"You're so rude! You've only known me for a few weeks. You don't even know how old I am. How could you ever know the foundations of my happiness?"

"Your unwillingness to test aspects of it tells me all I need to know. See, because you're not alone in that. Most people are like that. A relationship's probably the most important enterprise a person will ever undertake. I'm always amazed how people do more prep work before buying stuff like cars than they do before taking a relationship to another level." She glances up at the ceiling. "Take this place," she says. "Before we got this place, we had a survey done which involved people coming in and thoroughly checking the place over – the walls, the ceiling, the very floorboards we're standing on."

"Well, they clearly didn't do a great job. This place creaks when the wind blows!"

"Then they went to the non-physical stuff – checking titles and previous ownership and stuff . . . And that's for an inanimate object like a house. But the thinking was, if you're going to be paying for it over twenty-five years, then you'd better be sure about what you're getting into."

"I've known my Cyrus ten years, Lindsay. I think that's enough time to do the prep work, as you call it. I've been doing it since I was near an infant. Besides, look who's talking! How many marriages has it been? So far?"

"I haven't said I'm not willing to learn. I haven't claimed to be perfect on this. But it's about you now. Do you know what to look for? I've known you for six weeks and I know more about you than you perhaps know about him."

"Like hell."

"And why? Because I know what to look for now, that's why."

"You do?"

"Don't doubt it. Perhaps I exaggerated on the length of time I said it'd take for me to get into his pants . . ."

"Oh. So, longer than ten minutes now, is it?

"Perhaps. I'm saying, give me half an hour and that's the maximum it would take me."

"I suggest you stop drinking right now," Sabrina advises her.

Lindsay jumps to her feet. "Let's put it to the test, Sabrina! He should be due here any time now. We can work something out."

Sabrina lowers her head. "I'd better be going. Work's over. I won't be hanging around here."

Lindsay waves her off dismissively. "Yeah, run away. Don't mind me. I blame it on my farm upbringing."

"Your coarseness?"

"No, my tendency to realism. My aversion to mental cosmetics."

"Because you're so very strong, right?"

"No, listen. I'm being modest I'm calling it a gift and a curse. An accident of birth."

"Wonder how ready you'd be to look at your own life in the same way," spits Sabrina.

"Don't get me wrong. I'm always ready to put the laser

to my own life. And I do. As I said, it's all down to my farm upbringing. I think all that inoculated me against the blight that afflicts your generation."

"My generation? You sound like a sociology teacher. What are you – ?"

"Well, just not your generation. Everything in our culture conspires to prevent us gaining any realistic perspective on life. You know, last month we ran an article on the increased levels of mental illness among under-twenty-fives in urban areas? In the last five years, the level has increased by twenty per cent. Do you wonder why that is?"

Sabrina checks the time on her phone. "I can't say it is an issue that keeps me awake at night, Lindsay."

"Well, I think – "

"Because, nowadays, people are more aware of these things and more willing to do something about it? We've got the services now, Lindsay. We've – "

She cuts Sabrina off. "Only true in part. With the education and culture we feed to the young, it's inevitable they're going to end up disturbed, disappointed and confused once they bump their heads into reality."

"Are you saying I'm disturbed?"

"You're personalising. I'm talking more generally and all I'm saying is we feed people a warped view of the world. The culture we're fed's all geared to the sugar-coating of reality. I don't doubt that it's a necessary thing for youth – to a degree, but the pendulum's gone too far."

"You've definitely been on the sauce too early, woman. You did mention a taxi, didn't you? Because I hope you're not thinking of driving wherever you choose to go."

"We've come up with all these religions, all promising eternal life in one way or other, religions that people kill each other over, simply because people can't face the fact that it's the end of the road when we go."

"I'm going to call you a cab, because you're pissed and you're becoming morose."

"And then we have romance . . ."

Sabrina reaches for her phone again.

"And the huge industry it's spawned, with poetry, films, plays, just because we're too ashamed to admit that really, really, all we want to do is fuck."

Sabrina turns her back on her, the better to concentrate on her conversation with the mini-cab operator.

"And history. You don't have to travel long or very far to find it's just a bunch of lies to make people feel better about themselves. If you've got any kind of intelligence – these inventions can only protect you for so long."

"Lindsay, you're preaching. You obviously have your way of looking at things. And it's brought you to where you are."

Lindsay stops for a moment. "Are you judging me, Sabrina darling?"

Sabrina shakes her head.

"So, what's this 'brought me to where I am'? 'Brought me to where I am'? What does that mean?"

"No. We are where we are. I was talking in the broad sense."

"Do you not agree with me?"

"Do I have to?"

"If you can't see what I'm talking about, Sabrina, then you need more help than I imagined you do. OK, you say you expected to learn something from me. I'll tell you this one thing . . ."

"Do you have to? I'd rather you told me something when you're sober. I'd appreciate it more, then."

"I couldn't be more clear-headed. In vino veritas!"

Sabrina glances at the clock on her mobile phone again. "Really, now, though. I have to meet Cyrus at the bottom of the road."

"The most intense pleasures you can get are the pleasures derived from life itself, in the raw. But you've got to be brave to enjoy it. Because life itself can be harsh when you see it too clearly. It's why we feed kids fairy tales and censor their intake till they're old enough to see life in the raw. Only then do we disabuse them of all these fictions. But you're an intelligent girl and knowledge is there for the intelligent. And knowledge is the enemy to defences based on dodgy foundations. Knowledge is the enemy because knowledge can strip the protection down in an instant."

"You're crazy and drunk and wrong," Sabrina informs her. "And I'll show you how wrong," she adds.

Lindsay brightens. "You want to take the challenge?"

"The challenge?" repeats Sabrina. "You make it sound like a game. It is a game to you, isn't it? A game!"

"Well, yeah. In part. But for you it can also be an education."

"Oh, it will be. It will be."

"What's the forfeit?"

"What do you mean?"

"If I'm right, then you've got to come out with me tonight. It'll be our girls night out. And you've got to dress properly."

"Properly?" questions Sabrina.

"Yes, like a girl. Not an unemployed yob."

"I always dress properly."

"Well, let's just say if I win I get to pick every item of your clothes. If you're going out with me, you'll have to dress exactly the way I want you to dress. Stand right here. I think we're the same size. What size shoe do you take?"

"Five."

"You might have a squeeze."

"I'll have nothing of the sort, I reckon."

"We'll see. And what do you want?"

"What do I want?"

"In the unlikely event he keeps his drawers on. You name it."

"Nothing."

"You thought about that?"

"Uh-huh. I'll take nothing. Not even the pharaoh head. I'll get all the satisfaction I need from proving you wrong."

"OK. Let's set to it, then. Where were you going to meet him?"

"Bottom of the road."

"Text him to meet you here at the house. Text him the address." Her eyes survey the room. "I'll perform in here and you watch from the back room. He won't know you're there."

Slowly, almost reluctantly, Sabrina pulls out her phone and starts on a text message. Lindsay looks over her shoulder for a second then loses interest. She exits the room to get changed. Sabrina stares at the phone and considers calling Cyrus to provide him with some background. But she fights the urge. Her eyes rest on the array of alcohol in the wine rack. Lindsay re-enters the room about five minutes later. Her seduction outfit is a slight modification of her earlier costume. Now she wears a light-pink frilly blouse with the red skirt. The red heels remain the same. Sabrina stares expressionlessly at her for a full minute. Then she breaks the silence.

"They're all that simple, eh?" she says.

"Haven't you found?"

"Haven't had a chance to go through them all."

"Listen and learn. You see, these are the pressure points." She points to her crotch and then her head. "The dick and the ego. So for us it's all about physical display and flattery."

"That's all very good. If you can define half the human population in a sentence."

"Listen – " she begins, but Sabrina stops her.

"Before this kicks off, I do have a few ground rules," Sabrina tells her.

"Oh yeah?"

"I do."

"Like?"

"Like, no alcohol."

"For whom?"

"For him. You can carry on getting as pissed as you like."

Lindsay considers. "But that's no real test for him. In our world you'll find booze everywhere you go. Everywhere. If this exercise is going to be any good to you, we're going to have to simulate real-life conditions. If you don't want to expose your boy to situations where there'll be booze and women around, you'd better keep him hidden down those baggy trousers of yours."

"If this exercise is going to be any good for me? Let's not make out this has anything to do with my benefit. Please."

"Well, it has. It really has." She glances at her watch. "Have you texted him the right address?"

"You want to win your bet so you can have someone to go out with tonight and you want to rub my nose in it."

"Oh, you do think badly of me," Lindsay whines mock-woundedly on her way to the wine rack again.

Sabrina ponders a moment, then, "OK, fine. You can both drink," she concedes. "But you're not to touch him first. You can say what you want – you can wiggle your arse like a go-go dancer – but you're not to touch him first. If you do, then the whole thing's off. I'm not kidding."

"Yeah, wait. I've got a few ground rules, too."

"You have?"

"I have."

"Like?"

"Surprised, huh?"

"What are they?"

"Well, I've never seen this guy of yours."

"OK."

"I've just heard about him. And, strange as it might seem to you, given my mouth and what you've seen here, I haven't been fucked for more than three weeks."

"God, you're a disgusting woman!"

"So . . ."

"Yeah?"

She advances slowly to Sabrina. "So, if I like the look of him – this boy of yours – when he walks in . . ."

"You're a disgusting woman."

"And he ends up acting in the way I expect him to . . ."

"Not going to happen."

Lindsay turns away. "Well, you're not to come out here till the whole thing's run its course."

Sabrina is at a loss for words.

"Do you agree?"

"I don't know."

Lindsay glances at her watch again. "Well, you haven't that much time to think about it, really."

"The more I think about it . . . It's just not relevant."

"Hah. You don't think so, eh? No, but I do like confidence. It's going to make your lesson all the more important. Can I take it you don't disagree, then?"

"Whatever."

"OK. We've got agreement. But if I feel I don't want to fuck him, I'll knock hard on the wall or on the floor with the closest object to hand. Three times in succession. That will be your cue."

At this moment, Sabrina shakes her head in disbelief at what she, in relatively sober mind, has helped set in train.

Lindsay interrupts her thoughts. "What do you think of the way the dress hangs?"

"The truth?"

"No sugar-coating."

"You look like a geriatric stripper, Lindsay."

"It's your apprehension talking. So I won't take offence."

"You think so?"

"You won't begin to understand this yet."

The front doorbell rings and they regard each other in silence. The bell rings again.

"That's Cyrus," says Sabrina.

Lindsay leads Sabrina into the back room. It's a room that has always remained locked in the time she has worked here. It's simply furnished, with just a bed and a chest of drawers on which rests – to her great surprise – a small television. She turns it on and the image of the recently vacated living room presents itself on the screen.

Sabrina gulps in astonishment. "What is this?"

"From here, you can watch the whole thing."

"Fuck, Lindsay!"

"What?"

"You bitch!"

"What?"

"Have you been using this thing to spy on me? While I've been working here?"

"Initially, yeah."

"Bitch!"

"For the first week, yeah. With me not around sometimes, you didn't think I'd have someone wandering around my home for any length of time, did you? Someone who I wasn't sure I could trust?"

"I'm not employed as a fucking nanny, bitch."

"I've had some bad experiences. This is London. Get over it."

"I'm fucking speechless, Lindsay."

"Well, keep that up for another half-hour, will you?"

"Yeah, you've got half an hour. As soon as thirty minutes have gone, I'm stepping out of here and I'm ringing the front doorbell."

The doorbell sounds again. Lindsay leaves the room. Sabrina sits for a moment with her head in her hands until distracted by footsteps against the hard floor.

Cyrus appears on the television screen. He's wearing a black jacket with a blue T-shirt underneath.

"Where's Sabrina?" he asks. His voice sounds low and faintly distorted. Sabrina searches the room for the volume controls.

"Sabrina's not here," she hears Lindsay say.

Cyrus shuffles his feet. "Right. I got a message to meet here."

Sabrina grabs the pillow from the head of the bed and covers her face in shame. She remains motionless for a second, as if her mind is unable to catch up with recent discoveries and the speed of events she's voluntarily set in motion.

"She's kindly gone to pick something up in the West End for me," she hears Lindsay respond. "Should only take her twenty minutes on the bus to get there – and twenty back. But it's rush hour, isn't it?"

Sabrina glances back at the screen in time to see Cyrus look at his watch. "Well, just gone. There was an accident near . . ." He tries to remember the spot, but breaks off the sentence.

"No one hurt, I hope?"

"Dunno," says Cyrus. "Just heard the sirens, saw loads of police vans and ambulances. Delayed the bus."

"That's awful. Well, Sabrina said she'd text you that she'll be late and to meet her here. So, take a seat."

Cyrus takes a step to the sofa, then stops. "Look, maybe I should just come back later," he says.

"You sure?"

"Yeah, I'll come back in a mo." He steps away to the door and Sabrina rises from the edge of the bed and places a tentative finger on the television's on/off button.

"Yeah, no problem," he adds.

Lindsay stops him before he gets to the door. "One second," she says. "Before you go . . ."

"What's up?"

"I've got a little job needs doing."

Sabrina retreats from the television, grabs the pillow again and covers her mouth with it. It is all she can do to stop herself laughing out loud. At the same time, she fights back a surge of guilt at having agreed to put Cyrus through this.

"Yeah?" he asks.

"Hope you don't mind," says Lindsay and she moves, as languidly as her befuddled brain allows, to the middle of the room.

"What is it?" asks Cyrus.

"Hate to sound old-fashioned. But it's a job for a man, really."

Cyrus has a mystified look on his face. "Well, I'll see what I can do," he promises hesitantly.

"Wait here one moment."

Lindsay returns to the room with what appears to be an oval-shaped container. The picture on the set isn't so clear and the dim lighting in the room does not help. Lindsay hands it over to Cyrus, who regards it suspiciously at first.

"I'll be forever in your debt if you can crack that open for me," she says.

Cyrus begins tentatively by simply holding the object as if making a mental assessment of the task ahead. He then sits down with the item between his thighs as he tries to prise it open with his hands. Lindsay waits. She stands there with feet planted wide apart and hands on hips. He glances nervously up at her before shifting the container from the chair to the floor between his own feet. He then has another few unsuccessful attempts at pulling the lid open, until frustration clouds his demeanour. He glances up at her a few more times, then, inflating his chest once again, he has another go. This time Sabrina watches the lid come away in his hands. Lindsay takes a step back.

"Oh, great! You're a star!"

"No worries."

"You seem to have worked up a sweat there," she laughs, gently touching his brow, then springing back another step.

"Was tougher than it looked," he laughs nervously.

"Obviously. Did you think I was kidding when I told you it was a job for a man? Don't know what I would have done without you."

Sabrina winces. Some core part of her is crushingly disappointed at what she is seeing. So far, it has been a performance as cliché-ridden as the television shows she professes not to watch.

"That's OK," drawls Cyrus.

"Can I fix you a drink or something?"

"Er . . ."

"You might want to get your energy back."

Cyrus regards Lindsay in silence for a pregnant few seconds. "That's alright. I think I'll go and come back later."

Sabrina suppresses a giggle.

"But it's not a problem," Lindsay assures him. At that point, she strikes a pose that Sabrina expects she considers alluring: her head tilted back, her hands on her hips. "But if you insist . . . All I'm saying is, she'll be back before long."

"You sure?"

"Of course I am." She points to her travel bags. "I'm about to go out myself, so you're not treading on my toes in any way."

"Sure it's OK?"

"You're such a worrier. It's not a problem. It's better than you wandering the streets like a vagrant for an hour. Plus, I'd love to thank you for your help, at least."

Lindsay wiggles her hips on her way to the wine rack. Sabrina inches back from the television and to the edge of the bed.

"She's quite a girl, isn't she, Sabrina?" she hears Lindsay say.

"She is, yeah."

"I'm going to miss her. You know it's her last day working for me?"

"I think she mentioned something about that."

"Yeah, it's her very last time here with me. And I'm never going to see her again."

"Well, I'm sure she'll pop down and see you some time. She's good at keeping in touch."

"All the way from East London where she lives? I doubt she likes me that much." She hovers over a bottle of wine. "I couldn't even persuade her to come out with me tonight. Anyway," she sighed, pointing back to her suitcases again, "I'll be leaving soon."

"Where're you going again?"

"For a long break. Then god knows what I'll do after that. So, the chances of me and Sabrina meeting up again are going to be slim."

"When are you leaving?"

"Uh?"

"When are you leaving?"

"Early tomorrow. I'm guessing you're a vodka rather than a wine drinker."

Cyrus hesitates for a second. "Ah, whatever."

Lindsay sashays past him on her way to the kitchen. "Nothing to keep me here, see," she trails. Then her voice comes through faintly. "I've quit my job. I'm near enough divorced. Now single. There's this house. I could show you around in a mo." She returns to the room. "It's a bit large for little me, I reckon – so I may let it out." She hands him a drink. "I'm sure others could fill it better than I can."

"Where did you say you were going?"

"Around Morocco, mainly. But hope to stop off in Hurghada for a few days. Only decided three weeks ago."

"Short time for such a big step."

"You think so? Why?" She's standing before him, glass in hand.

"Well, it's another continent, another culture. If it was me . . . I'd take my time to work out the pros and cons . . . what I'm going to do . . ."

"I've forgotten your ice, haven't I? Give me your glass."

"Have you been there before?" he calls after her.

"Yeah, I went there for my first honeymoon."

"Still a big step, though," he says, raising his voice so that it carries to the kitchen.

She says nothing for a while, but saunters back to him, glass poised between her fingers.

"The moment's all we have in life," she eventually says. "Just the moment." She hands him back his drink, this time with ice. "You've got to grab it."

He looks up at her. Sabrina cannot tell if he's smiling "I've heard that said."

"I may not look like a candidate to be giving life lessons to anyone," begins Lindsay. "But what I've found, in my personal experience, is that nothing pains more than a missed opportunity. Have you not found?"

Cyrus shrugs. "Hope you don't mind," he says, "but I've just got to cut in and say this. You know who you remind me of?"

"Careful now."

He smiles. "No. No. It's just my opinion."

"Tell me. Who do I remind you of?"

"Shenka Lubal."

"The . . ."

"Yeah . . ."

She takes a sip of her drink and reflects. "I'm flattered. Very much flattered. You think we look alike, do you?"

"Well, the shape, the face," he pauses. "The . . ."

Lindsay waits expectantly. "The . . . ?"

He waves one hand dismissively, smiles and lowers his eyes. "Just all round how you come over. I don't know specifically why . . . Surprised you've heard of her, actually. She's not that popular in this country."

"There's even more to me than meets the eye, see? What'd do you think of the way she went to the press about that Gilberto Molina affair?"

"You mean with that politician?"

"A mayor, I think he was."

"Nothing, really. Happens, don't it? Maybe she felt hard done by and wanted revenge. Everyone's at it nowadays." Then, as an afterthought, "But the press over there lapped up the story, then they hammered her for giving it to them."

"Hmm, yes."

"She definitely came off even worse than he did."

Lindsay rises from her chair again to go to the kitchen. "But then again," she calls out on her way, "maybe she deserved it – in a way. You know, some people deserve a good hammering some time."

"Not like . . . Well, it's clear, if you follow how it went down, the American people definitely prefer him to her."

"Maybe they turned against her," she says as she comes back with a refilled glass.

"You reckon?"

"For what she did. Divulging intimacies, you know. Even where I come from, there was a certain code when it came to what went on between two people. So down to this day, I always believe that certain things between two adults should remain private. That's just what I believe, anyway." She pauses. "And you?"

"Well . . . yeah."

"I've always believed that . . . what goes on between two people should always remain between those two people."

"Well, you're right."

They sip their drinks together in silence. The silence lasts so long that Sabrina feels compelled to raise the volume on the monitor.

Cyrus is first to speak. "So," he says.

"So."

They both laugh.

"So, what made you decide to go to Morocco?" asks Cyrus. He takes off his jacket and places it over the armchair.

"Well, I recently came into a bit of money. And time. So, the chance came about."

"That's it?"

"Simple as that."

"And you're taking it. Of course."

"You've got to take it."

"That's right. Grab the moment."

"You're learning."

Cyrus points to the wine rack. "Do you mind if I fix myself another?"

"Sure. Get yourself something nice," she suggests to him as she heads to the kitchen again.

Cyrus glances at his watch. "So," he begins, when Lindsay returns and eases herself on to the sofa. "I was wondering er . . ."

"What were you wondering, tell me?"

"Er what accounts for you being so spontaneous?"

Sabrina sinks her face into the pillow.

Lindsay shrugs. "What accounts for anything we are eh?"

"I guess so."

"I tell you what though," she adds with a flourish. "I find phrenology and physiognomy to be fantastic indicators. Of what a person's like, I mean."

"Physiognomy" he repeats.

"Have you not heard of it? Where you can determine the character of a person just by their body shape;their physical attributes?"

"Oh yeah? I think we did that."

"You did that in your school?"

"College. They used it for criminals, didn't they? But I thought it was only the heads they done." He pauses. "But it didn't catch on, I didn't think."

"Its time hadn't come."

"So, what does your physical shape say?"

"My physical shape? Well, different parts signify different tendencies, see."

"OK."

"Of what's visible . . ."

"What story do your legs tell?"

"Well, legs are complicated because, unlike the head, people can change the shape of other parts of their bodies more easily."

Cyrus gently reaches out and touches Lindsay's leg. "So is this the work of nature or hours in the gym?"

"Oh, all my mother's work," she assures him with a lingering smile. "They say slim calves denote someone of even temper and appetites . . ."

Cyrus keeps his hands on her leg. "And what about women with . . . more convex calves? What does that tell me?"

"My reading didn't extend to that. So maybe you'll have to do some independent research."

Sabrina rises from the edge of the bed. A sense of revulsion and terror constricts her chest.

"That means I might have to do some investigating," smirks Cyrus.

"What I do know, though," begins Lindsay, "is that people who have naturally out-of-proportion legs . . ."

"Naturally out-of-proportion legs?"

"You know, lower leg disproportionately bigger or smaller compared to the thigh, or vice versa?"

"Yeah?"

"Well, these people can have great success but mainly in the second stage of their lives, from their thirties onwards, say."

"There's obviously some investigation work to be done. Because of the gap in your knowledge on the shape I mentioned."

"My shape?"

Lindsay is off to the wine rack again. Sabrina watches Cyrus fidget as he waits for her to return to him.

"Your leg shape," she hears him call out to her. His every word adds to the growing wound that is her pride.

"But it's your shape I'm interested in," Lindsay responds in a lilting tone.

"What's it say to you?" he asks.

She comes back towards him with a full glass of wine and considers him from a distance of two paces. "Well, let's see. Your head shape . . ." She places her hand at the back of his head, and to Sabrina's horror she sees him relax his limbs as if he'd surrendered himself to her completely.

"Musical talent, I'd say."

"You'd say that?"

"I would say that."

"You into music?"

"Isn't everyone?"

Cyrus rises abruptly from the sofa and walks over to his jacket.

"Where are you going?" asks Lindsay.

"I've got a mix tape here."

"Your own stuff?"

He glances at his watch. "Yep."

"Happy with it?"

"Dunno – well, I don't know how much you know about . . . but it's dance music. Got some slow jam instrumentals on there, as well."

"Slow jams. Right."

"And with this type of music you never know if it's good or not till you hear it in a club or see how it works when people actual dance to it. See how people feel it."

"OK." She regards it warily. "Why do you call it a mix tape when it's in fact a disc?"

"I dunno." He points to the CD player in the corner of the room. "Is that player working?"

"I think so. Haven't used it in a while."

"Can I have a try?"

"Be my guest."

Cyrus struggles with the CD player. "Don't take this the wrong way," he begins. "But I wonder what you spend your money on. Someone with your means really should be doing better with the electronic stuff in here."

Lindsay steals a discreet glance at her watch. "I know," she concedes.

With the disc finally in place, Cyrus stands back as the music floods the room.

"So?" says Cyrus, regarding her with what Sabrina discerns as a grin. He then holds out his arms.

"Are you going to sing along to me?" Lindsay asks.
"We can see how it works?" he suggests.
"We could do."
Cyrus advances towards her.
She holds out her arms. "As you wish."
Cyrus and Lindsay dance. Cyrus tries to move his face closer to hers as they move across the floor. At length, he pulls her on the sofa and climbs on top of her. She resists but he is insistent. He tries to kiss her mouth. She turns her face to give him her cheek instead. She whispers something into his ear but he continues his attentive efforts. She whispers into his ear again. This time he slides off her. Sabrina can't hear their voices now above the sound of the music. Lindsay motions him to remove his top. He regards her with some initial scepticism but slowly he begins to peel off his T-shirt. Then, quite suddenly, he jumps on her again.

It's all Sabrina can stand. She turns the television off. She sinks on to the bed, overcome by waves of grief, shock and shame. She fights the impulse to simply leave the house right away. There's a rap against the wall. This jolts her out of her uncertainty and she sits bolt upright. Seconds later there's another series of raps. Lindsay is calling. Should she ignore her? She now suddenly feels an inexplicable compulsion to see the tail-end of this brutish two-hander live and unmediated by pixels, speakers and cathode rays.

She stumbles out of the back room. In the corridor she pauses to take a deep breath and then she enters the scene. She meets Lindsay's eyes first. She's lying face up on the sofa with Cyrus on top of her. She holds her stare.

When Cyrus notices Lindsay's distracted gaze, he pauses his hip rotation and turns and observes his girlfriend staring down at him. He grimaces like some kid staring into the light. Sabrina turns her back on them and clasps her head in her hands, as if she's witnessed the gory aftermath of an accident.

Cyrus slides off the sofa and rises slowly on to his feet. Lindsay steps over to the CD player and turns off the music. She then moves over to the wine rack, with a disconcerting poise, given the quantity of alcohol she's had.

"Sabrina?" she asks.

Despite her best efforts, Sabrina hears herself weeping. Her shoulders heave and the tears flow down her cheeks. Lindsay, bottle in hand, edges away to the far corner of the room.

"Do you want a moment together?" she asks.

"No, stay!" Sabrina thunders. "Don't leave."

"Are you quite sure?"

Sabrina is trying heroically, to compose herself. "Yes, I'm sure," she says in a trembling voice. "In fact, I'm going to leave." She pauses to dry her eyes. She is shuffling to the door when Lindsay calls out to her.

"Right now, you're entitled to be emotional," Lindsay says.

"I'm fine," replies Sabrina. She cannot bring herself to look at Cyrus. "But I'd really prefer to leave – now."

Lindsay stops her again. "It's easy to forget our obligations when we get emotional. But we did have an arrangement. Now, if you're telling me you're unable to meet your obligations . . ."

Sabrina freezes. She remains motionless for half a minute, then sniffs loudly. "No, I'm fine," she eventually says. "What do you want me to do?"

"Nothing," says Lindsay. "Only what you want to do." She approaches Sabrina with her arms outstretched.

Sabrina shrugs her off. "Really, I just want to go home," she tells her.

"Now, I know you don't feel too good right now. But try to see it as a rite of passage. Like Santa Claus and tooth fairies, male fidelity was another fiction you needed gone my girl. There'll be others."

She feels Cyrus's eyes on her, but she still cannot bear to look at him. In her peripheral vision, she sees him move.

"Sabrina," he begins. "Sabrina, I – "

Lindsay interrupts him. "I know you feel raw right now, Sabrina. You wouldn't be normal if you didn't."

"Sabrina," he calls. "Can I talk to you?"

"But as I say," continues Lindsay, "it's all part of the growing process. The way a kid's got to lose baby teeth so stronger ones can grow in their place? Might be inconvenient for a while, but it's all for the good." She tugs at Sabrina's arm. "Sabrina, at some stage you had to be disabused of . . ." she breaks off. "Just call this a controlled disabusement of these fictions."

Sabrina's head is bowed and her eyes cast to the floor, but when she feels Cyrus's hands close around hers, she pulls violently away.

"Easy now," says Lindsay. "Don't be too mad at him. I can understand you being mad at him, but it's not totally his fault really, now, is it? You projected all these qualities on him to make yourself happy. Don't blame him because he couldn't live up to them. You can't blame him because he chose to act the way he was designed to. You can't blame a dog for being a dog."

"OK," says Sabrina. "What do you want me to do?" And the new resolve in her voice surprises both herself and Lindsay.

"Again, I don't want you to do anything you're not up to."

"I'm OK," she tells Lindsay.

"Are you sure?"

"Sure."

"What I recommend, though, is that you go out where there's people and light, have a chat, get drunk, and by tomorrow your perspective will be better than it is right now. I promise you. Are you up for that?" she asks, amused at how she catches herself slipping into the slang of her young companions for the evening.

Sabrina nods in her direction.

"You sure?"

"I'm ready. Let's get out of here."

"Now, one thing first. You know what I'm talking about, don't you? Yes, you do. Now, I think we share the same size."

Cyrus seizes Lindsay's hand authoritatively. "I want to speak to Sabrina. Alone," he says.

Lindsay turns to Sabrina. "Do you want some time alone?" she asks. "With him?"

"Please," Sabrina tells her. "Let's get out of here."

"OK. Upstairs with you! I'll have you dressed to reflect your new-found maturity."

Sabrina leads the way and Lindsay follows her without

a glance back at Cyrus. Once out of the door, Lindsay takes the lead up the stairs, yanking Sabrina behind her.

The feeling Sabrina experiences as she gets dressed by Lindsay is of being a spectator in a show involving her own life. During Lindsay's wine-fuelled commentary and oration, Sabrina's attention lies elsewhere, reviewing what played out in that malefic room downstairs. All the while Lindsay speaks, Sabrina listens in vain for that click that will let her know that Cyrus has finally left the house.

When they return to the living room, dressed up, they find him still seated on the sofa.

"Like a woman reborn," says Lindsay pointing to Sabrina's red blouse and long black skirt. "What'd you say, Cyrus?"

"Can we go now?" interrupts Sabrina petulantly.

"You're going nowhere," he says.

Lindsay regards him with a leer. "I beg your pardon?"

"You heard. You're going nowhere! None of you!"

Cyrus marches to the door and closes it firmly. He then marches to the curtains. He grabs a couple of rope tie-backs. He strides purposefully towards Lindsay who, unmoved, stares him down challengingly. He stands before her in silence for a moment. Then, in a sudden, smooth movement, he grabs her wrists and throws his weight against her, so that she falls on to the sofa. The shock causes her to give a high-pitched shriek. He presses his weight against her kicking legs till he secures a section of rope tightly around her wrists. Her shouts become deafening. Sabrina watches on – her expression, one of mixed incredulity and helplessness. With Lindsay's hands bound, he reaches for and uses the other rope tie-back as a gag for her mouth. Sabrina is thrown by the sudden drop in sound level as, within an instant, Cyrus's panting becomes the room's dominant sound – Lindsay's shrieking now replaced by her intermittent and muffled groans. He turns his gaze to Sabrina.

"Can you remove that thing from the woman's mouth and grow up?" she shouts at him. "I'm almost fucking embarrassed for you. She's choking!"

Lindsay slides from the sofa and slumps to the floor.

"She's turning purple!" Sabrina screams at him.

"She's quieter, though."

"She'll be damned near silent in a minute!"

She barges past him in an effort to get to Lindsay. He pushes her away.

"Can't you see the woman's choking to death here? At least leave some space round her nose so she can breathe! Are you going to let her go?"

"Eventually, maybe. But for now she's distracted you enough."

BITCH BOY

Human Biology 9.15 – 10.15

Beeeach! Beeeeaaach Bwoy! I wasn't going to look around. I was going to keep staring ahead at the blackboard until Sir put the chalk down, turned and got on with the lesson. Beeaaaaaaacccch Bwoy! Hey Bitch Boy. You na hear me call you? Beeeeeach! I would never answer to it. But I knew for sure, then, that it was a sticker. Round here, if two weekends go by and a name's still running on a Monday, then chances are you have to live with that name forever. Beeech Bwoy! Soon the older kids get hold of it; the younger ones; black kids, white kids, Asian kids; kids from the school down the road. It's a sticker. Attention, please. At last he was done at the board. You live the rest of your life with a fucked-up name. Concentration was shot. Sir stepped to the desk before him. It was covered in a black sheet. He clipped his fingers round the near edge of the black sheet and like a magician he suddenly lifted the sheet to reveal a browny-red thing lying on a large white plate. Ugh. What's that, Sir? You tell me. Can anyone help a classmate and tell him what that is? Sunday dinner! No, it's a heart, Sir. Correct. It's a mammalian heart. It's also something else, too. Yeah, manky! It's also one of the most efficient and important machines ever created. Was this Biology or Religious Studies? This region here is the atrium. I got to the classroom late, so I was stuck in the first row. Right up there, man. Still, though – could have been worse. At least I was at the end of the row. Window seat. And next to me was my best mate. It was his fifteenth birthday. After school he was going to have a party. He reckoned there'd be whisky and beer and vodka and some girls there. He didn't know, then, that I wasn't going to make that party. He agreed the name was a stinker. You can spend three years in a school slowly building a rep and something like that knocks you back to zero. One time you're popping like you own the place, the next you have Year 8 tossers giggling behind them hand in the corridors and tuck shop. He'd seen it go down. He said if I was in the final year I could let it slide. But he said living with a name like that for nearly two more years would be haaaard. He never said it straight but I know he believes I made it worse that day by not fighting back. But it would have been the same for anyone. Everyone knew Frank Latts was the hardest guy in the school. Settling the score with an evil breer like that – a breer whose drum is four doors from mine and who I've seen with my own eyes kick a guy hard in him head just for looking at him the wrong way; a guy for whom pain was nothing, who got the twins to slam his own fingers in a door just to get out of badminton class – is something you need to think about. Only one guy had ever won a fight with Frank Latts. But later, that guy nearly got merked. I'd rather have lost than carry round a face with scars like he had once Frank and his Staff had caught up with him. Can anyone tell me why the ventricles have thicker walls than the atrium? Top marks to the person who can tell me why the left ventricle has thicker walls than the right ventricle? No? Come on, guys, there was a clue to this last week! There's a clue from the subtitle on the blackboard. Look. Frank Latts was in my Religious Studies class that afternoon.

History 10.15 – 11.15

Between 264 BC and 146 BC a series of three wars took place between Carthage and Rome. At the time of the first war, Carthage had the largest navy in the ancient world. Rome, as you will recall from last week, had no navy to speak of. I was absent for the last lesson and so he wanted to speak to me after the end of the class. Normally, he was a safe teacher. But he was also my house-master and he took that kind of stuff very seriously. I got a back-row seat for this one and I was next to my best mate again. All I kept reminding myself as I sat there is how you don't gain and keep a rep the same way you move up the years in school; that is, just by having birth-days. A rep had to be fed all the time – the way your mum feeds the plants in the boxes on the windowsill. To feed it, you had to actually do things. And your peeps had to see you do these things. After more than a hundred years of tit-for-tat fighting against the Carthaginians, the Romans ensured a complete end to the bloodshed between the two polities. They razed the city of Carthage, slaughtered the inhabitants and ploughed salt into the ground so the earth would never feed survivors and future generations. And so ended the kingdom of the Carthaginians.

Sir? Oi, Sir! Yes, you at the back there? Sir, how does a kingdom start? Like how does a dude become king in the first place? As a result of his parents, normally. Have you heard of the word "succession'? But I mean the very first king, like before his father was king. Like before succession. We're veering off the point now, I'm afraid. That's for another lesson. Besides, as we learned three weeks ago, what system of government did the Romans have? It wasn't a monarchy. Can anyone remind me? A republic, Sir! That's right. A republic.

Break Time 11.15 – 11.30

My best mate slipped out the gap in the wire side fencing to sneak a fag. I wandered over to the front of the great hall. For the first time in the two weeks since it happened, I was at the spot in the playground where it had kicked off. The site where I'd lost my name. Now, on its own, a pasting from Frank Latts was not an unusual thing. It was something I had in common with dozens of guys every week. But I'd been unlucky. I'd been well unlucky. It'd been pissing down that break time when he'd shoulder-barged me. Hundreds of guys had been sheltering under the canopy bit of the great hall. I thought it had been one of the Year 9 guys who'd been messing about with a basketball earlier. When I felt the pressure, I turned around ready for a hook. But I didn't take a swing. He was with the twins and he was mad as hell. It wasn't just the beating.

It was the way the beating went down. I expected a right cross. The first blow came with his left, though. It turned out to be a slap and it took me by surprise. He used the back of his hand and he'd followed through, like he was a tennis player making a top-spin backhand. It wasn't that painful, but I'd hit the deck. I thought staying down a while would take the heat out of things and that he'd move on. But, with the rain and all, maybe it made it easier for him to just remain there standing over me. He was screwing that I'd even thought of taking him on. The crazy face on him! More guys came running to the spot. It brought out even more of the devil in him. And that's when he came out with it.

"Bitch Bwoy! Wha you gon do?" he'd said.

The whole playground fell silent. Even the rain had seemed to stop at that moment. They were checking for my move. I'm about the same size as Frank. Not as broad, but a bit taller. I remained on the deck, rubbing my cheek. It didn't hurt – just stung. I knew that if I got up, he'd only hit me again. So, I kept my eyes to the ground. To look at him would only have made him madder. But he was still mad as hell. Screwing.

"Cha! Just stay where you are, bitch boy!" I heard him bark. "Move one inch and me gan finish you right here!"

Some laughter. Giggling. Some groans of disgust. I glanced up. His fly was undone. He turned his head left then right to check he was clear of Sir's gaze. "Move one inch and your head's off your fucking neck!"

I heard the giggles grow in volume as I switched my gaze back to the ground.

"Nah, man, that's cold!"

"Raaaa!"

"Grimy."

I closed my eyes. And I did move. I covered my face with my hands. I wasn't getting his piss anywhere near my mouth or my eyes.

"Beeeaach!" He was zipping up with the twins a step behind him folded up with laughter. I got up right away and slid out of my wet, stinky blazer. I left for home. I didn't return for a week. I didn't sleep right for a week. A punch in the face, a smack in the chops, a head-butt to the forehead: anything would have been better than copping a slap like that, at that time and in that place.

Now, it was all about what happened from there. In a way, it was all about Errol, my younger brother. The only person I care about in the world now. The whole world, including my mum and all. Errol's starting here in September. I'll still have a year to do when Errol starts here.

Mathematics 11.30 – 12.20

I slid out a hole in the side fencing on the blind side of the school building. I headed for the shopping mall. Frank Latts would have been in Maths. I didn't want to lay eyes on that guy yet. There was no choice but to do this in school. Outside the school gates, his Staff was like a dog-shadow to him. Man, couldn't get close enough to lay a finger without that mutt clamping its jaws round you. Sparking him up in school would even the score a bit and claw me some of my rep back. But he was one evil breer. He wouldn't rest. He would come back for me.

This is something I kept thinking about a lot while hunched over a milkshake in McDonald's.

Lunch Break 12.20 – 13.10

From McDonald's, I legged it over to the drum. The second I opened the door, she called out my name. But with a question mark on the end. She shuffled into the corridor. She was surprised to see me. I was more surprised to see her. I thought she was on day shift. I told her I'd put the wrong books into my bag by mistake this morning. She stared at me. She sucked her teeth. She shuffled back into the kitchen. Mum is always angry. But I had to get into the kitchen for just long enough to do my tings. So, I was going to chill in the living room till I got my chance. Then, I had to shoot over to Errol's school. I didn't want the regret of not saying goodbye. My head hadn't yet hit the back of the living room sofa when she charged into the room again.

She held a carton of orange juice in her hand.

"What's that?" I asked her.

"You tell me what it is."

"I had a glass this morning."

"You had a glass?" She stared at the carton, then switched her eyes to me. "Well, me ketch you now. Look!" She was shoving the carton into my face. "And you can't say it was Errol, cos last night he stay with him father. Look!"

Now, she held the carton up to the light. "Yesterday me buy this! Me had one glass before me go to sleep. And you not gon make me believe in duppy here now!"

"I just had a glass before school this morning," I insisted.

She shoved the carton closer to my face and then she moved it up to the light that streamed through the net curtains. I leaned forward. Incredible. Last night, she'd taken the trouble to mark a short line, in red lipstick, against the level of orange juice she'd left in the carton that night. Fucking hell. I had nothing to say after that. And I didn't even try.

"I not going to let you drive me mad here," she continued. "I know how much I used to spend on shopping not so long ago. And I know how much I have to spend now, since you start with your fresh attitude. You not the only one who live here, you know! That you think you can eat down the whole place now and leave nothing for everyone else!"

That "everyone else" was interesting. Only me and her and Errol lived here. But she was off on one, calling me ungrateful and selfish and predicting that I'd have a different attitude to money when I was sixteen and started earning my own way. The woman was losing her mind.

I kept staring at the blank television. She was frothing at the mouth over nothing much. I was sure she kept a calendar in her room and marked off the days till I got to sixteen in the same way I used to mark down days to Christmas. The devil in me wanted to wind the bitch up even more; to tell her that she'd have even more than two years to put up with this. I could tell her I was going to stay on at school and that after that I was going to enter South Bank University; that I'd be poncing round here till I was twenty-one at least, reading textbooks and raiding the fridge while she did her shifts.

But she'd have exploded if I'd run a line like that. I didn't know what was wrong with me. Lately I'd go for a slice of toast and end up eating through half the packet before I felt better. Early this morning, I went for a sip of orange and before I knew it I'd emptied half the carton into my guts.

As soon as I heard her in the bathroom, I slid into the kitchen, pulled open the cutlery drawer and then I was ready for the afternoon. Her mood didn't suit a decent goodbye. I texted Errol to meet me at his school gate. I ran him some story about wanting to borrow some dough. He said it was cool. He was the best little brother any guy could wish to have. He was the coolest kid. He was so cool that I let it slide that even my mum preferred him to me. That's how cool he is.

He'd stayed at his dad's last night. You could tell because he was wearing brand new Nikes. I had to be careful how I played this. Anything too soppy and he'd only get worried. But this was a moment. And I recognised that.

He emptied all the change in his pockets into my hand and said he had to run off to an English lesson. I eyeballed him hard when I told him thank you. I told him to take care of himself.

Accounting 13.10 – 14.00

I got to the class late. I got a middle-row seat. Anything to do with words and I can find my way. But put figures in front of me and I start yawning like I've been given medication. It didn't help that it was hot as hell. But I had to keep my blazer on from now on. I'd been patting myself down every ten minutes. I was prepared. But there was still time to back out. I thought about the down sides of going through with this. Getting shift would be a sickener for Mum. But then again Her Majesty would be responsible for my meals for the next few years and Mum could use that dough on Errol or on her wardrobe instead. I've heard man say you can study in jail. I bet it'd be easier to concentrate in there than it is round here nowadays, for sure. There'd be no girls, though. Not for years. I'd be looking at getting my first piece of pussy in my thirties, perhaps. The thought almost brought tears to my eyes. It was a long time to be wanking. Not that I was getting any play on the outside, anyway. Not compared to the other guys round my way or some of the Year 12 guys who'd talk in the tea room at break time. Maybe I'd come out of jail hench and shit – like Earl Gomez's brother when he came out. I'd spend every day there in the gym and come out ready to make up for lost time.

And then again, I could let this whole Frank thing slide. I'd be disgraced for the next two years, but free. Errol would enter school in September as Bitch Boy's Brother. His inheritance from me. Bitch Boy's Brother. There's an even more terrible sound to that name. Bitch Boy's Brother. Man was going nowhere carrying a name like that on him back through him school days. I'd have to disown him for his own good.

Religious Studies 14.00 –

I was hearing nothing she was saying. For the hundredth time, I checked the time on my mobile. We were now halfway through the lesson. My palms were wet with my own sweat. My heart raced. All the same, I couldn't help marking this as the last lesson I'd ever have in school. If the god of school had offered me a final question to ask on this my last day of school, I would have asked Miss if it was always a mortal sin to merk a man – in all cases, every time one person took another person's life. Surely, it couldn't be a mortal sin to merk a bad person? Or why did we kill dictators or go to war with bad people? Or were these exceptions? And did these exceptions only count when you kill with government armies and not on your own? But I wouldn't ask her. I couldn't take the risk, then, that she'd give me the wrong answer. This was all about my personal freedom to do the right thing for me and my peeps.

The twins were seated on either side of him. When I stepped up, they were the first to look round at me. I stood waiting for Frank. I wanted his eyes. It was tricky because he had to see me for long enough to know who was merking him, but not long enough to be able to do anything about it. When I caught the whites of his eyes, I reached into my inside pocket. On the first blow, his hands flew up in the air. A splash of red striped his desk. He made a terrible, terrible sound that shit me up with its volume and paralysed me for a second. He tried to fix his hands round my wrist. After that first stab I really did struggle to get the blade out of his chest. But my eyes caught Miss Frith shooting for the door. Deafening shouts and screams. More feet towards the open door. I'd known concentration would be hard, so once I got the blade out I kept a rhythm going in and out of his chest. The twins were out of there. He slid from his chair and his head smacked the desk on its way down to the floor. I kicked the desk forward to allow us space on the floor. Now he was bloodied chest up. I kneeled over him. I continued my rhythm. I couldn't say how long my hands kept rising and falling towards his chest. His blood felt hot round my hand, dripping down my wrist. My head rose and fell in the stabbing motion and now each time my head rose I felt the brushing of fingers and knuckles against the back of my neck and flicking my ears. Some guys were getting too close with their mobile phones.

Yeah motherfucker! How you like that? How you like that eh? Yeaaaah! Right, left, right, left, right, left! Right ventricle! Left ventricle! Where's the Staff, man? Where's the fucking dog? Yeah! How many times? What's my motherfucking name now, Frank? What's my fucking name now, bitch! Scipio. Yeah. Scipio mutherfuuuucking Aemilianus! Take that you fucking piece of shit!

I tore into his chest and gut like under there, in his heart, his spleen, his liver, he'd buried my name. My proper name. And I was on a tight deadline to find it and get it back. He wasn't in good shape now. He lay there like a filleted fish. Now that his screaming had stopped, the clicking of the phone cameras kept growing next to my ears. My head came to a rest. I raised my hand one last time and then I dropped the knife so that the wooden handle thudded against his chest and fell to the ground. It had done its job. Like some conductor, it had sucked his rep through its blade and into my veins so that now, as I rose to my feet, all eyes were on me and no one even glanced at the blood-splattered face of Frank

Latts. I staggered backward till the back of my head smacked the blackboard. I stepped forward and glanced down at his pitted chest. Of those left in the room, I was still the only one looking at him. I posed for a final shot. I felt those left expected some words from me.

"Don't fuck with me!" I said. I intended a roar. It came out little above a whisper. Then, still breathing heavily, I shuffled out into the corridor, to wait.

I got restless. It was taking ages for a bloke in a suit to get there. And my mind got to running on all kinds of stuff. I headed up to the library. That packed corridor cleared of Year 12s like I was Moses before the Red Sea. I stepped into the library. On sight of me, two Year 11s dusted out of there. A globule of blood plopped on to the keyboard when I logged on to the computer. I passed my hand over my hair and got a new coat of blood on my fingers. The library window was open. Sirens outside the school gates. Then, quite suddenly, they stopped. I wiped my fingers against the underside of the desk. It felt rough. Smooth passage disturbed by dried chewing gum; stale bits of packed lunch; stalagmites of snot. I typed the phrases "murder" and "juvenile" and "jail term" into the search engine. I kept my eyes trained on the monitor and waited.

MEMORY STICK

Jake drummed his fingers against his notepad. He'd kept Tandy waiting an uncomfortable ten seconds for a response. The question came again.

"I asked if you went to the gym this morning, Jake."

Jake stiffened. His huge ears seemed to prick up and twitch. He considered Tandy with suspicion. "What are you getting at?"

Tandy was sitting across the conference table from Jake. He glanced at me first, then he cast his eyes upward as if beseeching the fluorescent strip lighting above for patience. "No, Jake," he replied calmly. "I'm just asking if you went to the gym earlier. I'm making conversation here."

"No need to get tetchy," I tried to assure Jake. I was seated on the far side of the table, the furthest away from the door. "Tandy's probably just noticed the wonderful glow about you this morning and he wanted to know whether it was down to your recent exertions in the gym."

"I'll put my foot up your arse in a minute, Ian," Jake said to me. He's a huge, taciturn man, ex-Navy and with an aggressive edge about him. His silver-rimmed glasses rested almost apologetically on the bridge of his bold nose.

Even through the lenses I saw that his eyes were red. Lack of sleep, I guessed. I'd heard how Jake's wife had given birth to a little girl last week.

Jake Reeves and Tandy Dickson were colleagues of mine. Jake was the senior trading consultant and Tandy was the commercial frameworks director. It was 12.10 p.m. on a Monday morning and we were in room 3.01 of Ensign Energy Trading in Canary Wharf. We were waiting to be graced by Kitson Jones, our managing director of the past six months. We'd been waiting for more than fifteen minutes now. Tandy rose from his seat to get himself a coffee from the low trolley positioned just inside the room. He wore a light-green tie that worried me. I'd bought an identical one months ago in a Buenos Aires back street, thinking to hand it to Dad as one of my Christmas presents. I thought it'd be original around here in England. I was tempted to ask Tandy where the hell he'd got it from.

He held up the steel-coloured jug. "Anyone?"

Jake shook his head and returned to drumming his fingers against his notepad. Between us we'd given thirty years to Ensign. Plans for company rationalisations announced to us last week meant two of the three of us would be getting the chop in six weeks' time.

"I'm going to have a quick ciggie," I told the others when I felt the buzz in my pocket and saw that you were calling to remind me I had to meet her at the apartment. I hadn't forgotten.

"He'll be here any second," warned Jake as I started off.

I ignored him and took your call outside the lifts. On my way back, through the glass doors, I caught sight of Kitson whizzing past. He came to a sudden stop when he saw me. He waited for me to open the door and he smiled, showing tiny, rat-like, teeth.

"How was your weekend?"

I told him it was one of those uneventful ones.

"Can you give my apologies to the guys?" he said. "But if I don't get a bun down me now, I'm going to collapse. I'll be five minutes." He showed me those teeth again, and he disappeared down the corridor with his overcoat in the crook of his arm.

"His Excellency says he's going to be another five minutes," I told the guys when I got back to 3.01. "And, cool as you like, he asked how my weekend was. Can you believe the guy?"

"Well, what'd you expect?" asked Tandy.

"Normally, if a guy out there does something that could stop you feeding your kids, paying your mortgage and clothing your family, you'd . . . Well, a guy like that wouldn't have the nerve to even try speak to you, much less exchange pleasantries or whatever . . . He'd know you wouldn't want him breathing . . ."

"It's not Kitson's fault," interrupted Jake, gruffly.

Tandy slurped his coffee. "If you think it's Kitson who hatched this up," he said, "you're as naive as a convent girl. He's only doing his job. It's the senior management team – more especially, it's the number-crunchers." He sized me up. "Besides, Ian, you don't have any kids."

A piercing sound had him jumping out of his Hermès shirt. Coffee leaped the lip of his cup and spilled on to the tabletop. Jake shot him a contemptuous look and then his eyes turned to the brown, oblong lake taking form on the conference tabletop.

"I guess the meeting's cancelled," I announced as I rose to my feet.

In seconds, transformed into fluorescent orange, safety-vest-wearing superheroes, the designated fire wardens, were poking their heads into the room. Tandy protested in vain that he wanted to take a leak first. At the far end of the corridor, bobbing heads were being shepherded towards the far-side steps. We were marched past the lifts, to the doors on the other side of the building. A procession was already making its way down to the exit. The tick-tack of heels on stone steps echoed against the walls. All the way down, the ticking was punctuated by shrieks and bursts of puerile laughter. I watched Tandy pause to fill his lungs with air as his Chelsea boots reached the foot of the steps and his fingers closed around the shiny metal fire-door handles. He seemed to be filling his frame with air to gird his spirits and to insulate him from the cold outside.

"Get on out there! Get on with it!" came the teasing calls from behind him.

I was hoping for the real thing and not one of those tedious fire drills we had to endure at least once a year. We began the slow trudge towards the corner of the road and into the courtyard. There, a placard-bearing warden denoted the assembly points for staff on each floor. I couldn't make out the floor numbers on the placards, so I simply followed Tandy's boots.

"Why do these things always happen on the coldest day of the year?" I heard the IT manager moan to my PA.

By now, the absence of sirens and fire engines confirmed my fears that this was just a drill. Scores of staff swarmed about the courtyard, seeking their positions before the correct placard denoting each of the four floors. Jake had already found his position before the Floor 3 placard. He was talking to one of the guys in his team, and all the while his huge head and raw ears proclaimed his presence perhaps as well as any register call could.

It only took a few minutes standing there with Tandy in the presence of the whole assembled company to make me feel self-conscious. The volume of the hubbub rose steadily. Increasingly, I got the feeling we were being stared at. I got the feeling we were being talked about too. I plunged deeper into the circle, like an emperor penguin who'd done his stint on the outside. My shuffling feet stopped at Seymour, my product services manager. He raised his head, smiled, and then lifted his left hand to his brow in a mock salute. Suddenly, he averted his gaze to give a lusty "Safe and sound!" as his name was called from the register.

"I want you to do me a favour," I told him.

He raised his brow in an exaggerated fashion. But he was listening carefully.

"I'm going to take the chance to slide off for an early lunch," I said. "I want you to send an email to the regulator attaching our consultation response on their proposed price control review. I marked some changes on your draft – just accept them and copy me in on the covering email."

A cackling laugh rang out into the cold, thin air. It was unmistakably Trevor Finch, the chief operating officer. He was in one of the circles a few paces behind us that also comprised the chairman and Kitson himself. Kitson had his hands stuffed into his overcoat pockets and was shifting his weight from foot to foot. He was looking up at the others as they spoke.

"So, you're sloping off?" questioned Seymour.

"In seconds."

"You're forgetting something."

"Yeah, what?"

"Your unfortunate surname?"

He must have read the expression on my face too clearly, because he blanched slightly.

"I mean, 'Wang' is obviously going be last on the register," he amplified. "It always is."

"That's the second part of the favour," I told him, and I watched a slow, apprehensive smile break out on his face. "Yep, I want you to shout out my name when he calls it. I've overheard your impressions of me near the water cooler, so I have confidence you can pull this off."

I was well thawed out by the time the taxi driver pulled up before your friend's ground-floor apartment. But I wasn't ready. I felt as erotic as a boiled egg as I plucked the keys from the concierge's fingers and went on inside. I hung my coat and jacket on the empty coat stand. I was almost an hour early, so I dragged my feet around the rooms. I felt like a golfer checking over the course before a tournament. With the place having been vacant for a while, I soon noticed how chilly it was, especially in the larger rooms. In the kitchen, I tried to get the central heating going but without success. For fear of damaging something, I left it alone, and I finally settled down in the bedroom. The walls were painted violet. A stringless cello rested on a chair next to the window.

Soon, my thoughts began to wander. I opened the A4 notepad I'd been carrying when the fire alarm had gone off and I settled into the red fabric armchair next to the king-size brass bed. Between the notepad's pages, I'd earlier placed a new trade magazine. I'd had an email ping-pong match with the editor over an article on transmission use of system-charging methodologies I'd written for them. As the deadline loomed, I'd thrown my hands up in the air and told him to write what he wanted if he felt that dumbing down the content and losing the sense of the piece would help his cause. I was expecting the worst from the text. What I wasn't prepared for was the photograph they chose to run with the article. It took me a couple of seconds to recognise the tight-lipped pompous twat as my good self. Of the ten shots I'd posed for, they'd picked the worst. And they'd probably used the fee I'd waived to retouch the shot and make me look like a clown. Hardly a calling card if things turned bad for me at Ensign. I struggled to beat back a rising and inappropriate tide of anger. I didn't trouble myself to even read the thing.

My next step was to retire to the bathroom. I had myself a piss, though I didn't really need one. While staring into the oval mirror above the washbasin, I washed my hands. Then I took a pace back, fished my knob out again and smeared the tip with some hand soap. I rinsed and examined it for a while. Then I glanced at my watch. It was a shame about the heating. It was hard to imagine that in less than twenty minutes the pitifully shrunken thing in my hands would be called upon to probe and pleasure a healthy, athletic woman. It seemed unlikely – like watching a Mini Cooper being revved up on the front-row grid at Monza. I zipped back up and stepped into the cramped living room. My eyes landed on the drinks cabinet and I poured myself a brandy, which I sipped straight. Looking for a mood-changer, I turned on the television and settled into the sofa. I switched to one of those R&B music channels. It was the closest I could get to porn at this time in the afternoon.

By the time I returned to the bedroom, I was calmer and my brandy glass was empty. I returned the magazine to the inside of the notepad. The hum of an engine brought me to the window. I looked out and saw a car pulling into one of the apartment's parking bays. I retreated a pace but kept peering through the gaps in the pattern of the net curtains. She stepped out of her magenta two-seater Maserati. I dashed back into the living room and turned the television off. I'd left the front door ajar, as you'd suggested.

When I got back to the window, she hadn't moved from the spot where she'd parked the Maserati. I watched her staring up at the apartments, presumably trying to read off the correct door number. She took a few hesitant steps forward. She was a brave woman. In the freezing wind, her legs showed bare beneath the long red coat that she wore. A burst of sunlight made her raise her hands to her face and I imagined for a second that she had spotted me at the window and had cupped her hands over her brow to better check it was really me. I backed off, all the while keeping my eyes on her until she started towards the front door. Something in her hesitancy, or in my being in a position to watch her indecision unobserved, stirred me to a place beyond arousal and almost into the realms of nausea.

I positioned myself at the edge of the bed. Too obvious. Way too obvious. I slid across to the armchair instead. I heard her shuffling around outside, and then the front door closed behind her. She came down the short corridor and I heard her movements in the living room. Then I heard her steps in the kitchen. The bedroom door was open and I was praying she didn't call out. That would spoil everything. For a fleeting moment, I regretted not having poured a brandy for her. She had to be at least as apprehensive as I was. Beyond the dos and don'ts you'd fired at me over the phone, I hadn't given much thought to how I was going to play this. One thing I had determined on was to keep smiling. So, she walked in to my smiling face. She gave a slight nod, and her gaze moved momentarily from my face to take in the bed, the walls and the lighting.

I thought then that some words might have been appropriate. Still, I was painfully aware the entire time how easily the slightest pleasantry could lead to a full-blown conversation that would break the spell and defeat the whole object of the meeting. Caution prevailed and I remained silent.

She gave a little "Hmmpf". She didn't take a further step into the room but remained there with her hands on her hips and her figure framed in the doorway. She shifted her gaze from my face to every part of the room but the bed. Her own face was now flushed.

I concluded that I had to make a move here. If I didn't, we could remain staring at each other till the sun went down. I rose from the armchair and, with my eyes fixed on her all the while, I took a couple of steps forward. I smiled again and she gave me a cautious but not discouraging look. I reached for the bottom button of her coat. She remained still as I worked on it. Then I tackled the one above. I raised my head to observe her face. She stared past me. I carried on upward. Her breathing was unsteady and anxious. Her low-cut black blouse was now visible to me and my hands might have lost some steadiness as I came to the finish. Only the top one remained when her hand slowly came down over mine. A cold clamp. I gave her a questioning look, and for the first time her bright brown eyes fixed me for longer than a second.

"This is no good," she said. She gently pushed my hand away.

We stared at each other for a moment. She turned on her heels and was making for the front door. I followed her for a few paces, then stopped. I wasn't sure where I'd left the keys. I returned to the room and dashed to the window in time to see her come into view, crossing the forecourt to her car. She sped away.

I remained rooted to that spot. I gazed out from that window for a long while. A sense of numbness possessed me. It was a call from Kitson that snapped me from my brooding. He claimed he'd hoped to carry on our meeting after the alarm had gone off. *Sure*, I thought to myself. *Sure you did.* He whined on about having to rearrange things and how his diary was already unmanageable. By then I was holding the phone well away from my ear. I took my time getting back to the office.

Even as I rode the lift to the third floor, I hadn't

completely shaken off the sense of regret that lingered about me. Before getting to my desk, I sought some distraction in having a chat with Jake. His back was to me as I approached the pod of desks and computers from which his team operated. The merits of open-plan office arrangements! The rest of his team had their heads down at their keyboards and I was hoping to peer over his shoulder a while to check if he was knocking out CVs. It'd be just like an ex-Navy man to be getting the lifeboats ready. Instead, I found him surfing the internet for North African winter holidays.

I was convinced that Jake held the clues to what was to pan out here. I was convinced of psychic abilities even he wasn't aware that he possessed. He didn't say much, but he was the kind of guy who would now and again make off-the-cuff statements about work or about forthcoming sports fixtures, and long after he himself had forgotten what he'd said I'd watch what he'd predicted come to pass. I'd mentioned this to Tandy, who had a more prosaic take on Jake's abilities.

"He's not the least bit psychic," he jeered. "It's just that he can't verbalise his rationalisations."

I begged to differ. For me, it was like those great ears of his were antennae or some kind of Wi-Fi, plucking from the ether signals outside the range of senses given to the rest of us.

This heightened sense alerted him to my snooping form behind him. His fingers froze on the keyboard and, without turning, he quietly asked me to fuck off. *Fool's paradise*, I thought to myself.

* * *

That evening I delayed my return home and stopped off in the betting shop for an hour. My limbs felt heavy, my head light. I put all the cash in my wallet on Arsenal to beat whoever they were playing in the Champions League in a fortnight. The sense of euphoria that revitalised me diminished in direct proportion to how close I got to the house, to be replaced by foreboding as I gained my front door. I'd been walking with my head to the ground for the last two hundred metres. The omens weren't good. On opening the gate, I raised my head and saw that another lot of graffiti had been daubed on both the garage doors. We'd only got rid of the last lot this month. As far as I could see, it was the same stuff as last time: a slogan by a local Bible-basher.

"Yeah, you saw it," she drawled, as I walked into the living room. She was lying on the sofa wearing trainers and jogging bottoms. "I told you we need to get cameras installed," she reminded me.

"Christian vandals," I muttered. "Who would have thought."

I was half-grateful for something neutral to talk about, like a goalkeeper getting a first touch on a ball to steady his nerves. She'd cooked goulash and dumplings for dinner and I dished it up while she continued watching some interminable celebrity competition, this time one set in the Australian jungle. While we ate, I silently rehearsed how I was going to raise the issue of this afternoon. But she had other stuff on her mind.

"I met Prakesh Patel," she called out to me matter-of-factly. I turned around and her eyes were still on the television.

"And who the hell is that?"

"From your work."

"I don't know him."

"Short guy. Birmingham accent. Engineer?

"Where?"

"In Tesco. I heard someone calling out, 'Rita, Rita', and I ignored him at first, till he tugged at my sleeve at the checkout."

"OK. How'd you know him?"

"Your last office Christmas do?"

"I can't even remember him being there."

Then she said it. "He told me you could be laid off," she said. She still hadn't looked at me. I saw her tilt her head down to her plate for a moment. Then, "Is it true?" she asked, looking up.

I could hardly believe what she was saying. My blood quickened. I felt a mixture of terror and relief. Since I'd been given the news more than a week ago, I'd been trying to catch her in the right frame of mind to let her know. I'd sat with her, staring at images on the television screen and hoping for a line of dialogue, a comment from her that would provide the cue. So after days of awaiting the right moment and even considering whether I needed to break the news – after hours monitoring her moods with the attention of a surfer for the right wave, after the rehearsals, the mental warm-ups and the aborted bedtime attempts – I'd finally been outed.

It took me a while to come up with some words. "It's a possibility," I coughed. "They're restructuring the team. They're going to amalgamate Jake's team, Tandy's team and my team into one." The further I went on, the bolder

I got. I pressed on. "So they'll have the lucky new director doing triple the work for slightly more dough." I carried my plate back into the living room.

"How's that going to work?" she asked. Her tone was more curious than concerned.

"Well, the three of us have to compete for the new role of product services director of the former three teams. They'll probably cut down the team members, as well."

"You'll get a payoff, though, right?"

"Well, no amount to talk about – given our monthly outgoings."

"You'll just move on, Ian."

"Would have been easy two years ago. No one's hiring now, though."

She examined my expression. "Are you worried?"

I shrugged.

"How're the others taking it?"

"I can't believe how calm they are. That's the one thing I can't get over." I'd slipped into thinking aloud.

"Everyone will be calm so long as they think they have a chance."

"Jake thinks he's got a good chance, being the longest-serving. Tandy thinks he's got a chance – doesn't think they'll dare sack the only senior ethnic executive in the company."

"Well, you're Chinese."

"Rita, I'm half-Chinese. It doesn't quite carry the same weight with the Commission."

"So how're they going to decide who stays?"

"A bush-tucker trial. See who can eat a kangaroo's nuts without puking."

She shot me an irritated look.

"No, they've set up an interview, including a presentation."

"A presentation?"

"Yep."

"You all have to do the same presentation?"

"Yep."

"And when's this interview? Or should I call it a shootout?" Only she was allowed levity in this matter.

"On the fifteenth of March," I told her.

"Mmm. That's almost a month away."

"It is. I guess they're hoping two of us do the right thing and jump ship. That would make things easier for them."

On that Wednesday evening, Rita announced she would not make our appointment with you. She didn't bother to provide a reason. So I was truly embarrassed when you called that day. I knew you were reminding me about the appointment but I didn't have a credible excuse. I didn't respond to your call. I let it go to voicemail and I went to the golf course instead. I'm sorry.

Two weeks before the big day, I returned to the office after a lunch break and through the glass doors outside the lift I spotted Tandy at my desk. He was speaking to two members of my team. He had his legs stretched out, feet crossed at the ankles, with his heels resting against the edge of the desk. I caught him in profile, all relaxed, with head tilted back, and he was making a great show of laughing at something one of them had said to him. Instead of heading left outside the door, I turned the other way and made for the toilets.

I was alone before the urinals. And once again I was taking a piss I didn't really need. But I wanted a quiet spot to compose myself after witnessing Tandy in that scene at my desk. While washing my hands, I hoped that by the time I got back he would have gone. But fearing he'd still be there – and he did look comfortable – I rehearsed before the mirror some expressions that would convey in a controlled and measured way, what I felt about this. In my head I also ran through possible opening lines. I was interrupted by a flushing toilet. Someone had been in one of the cubicles. I tried to recall if I'd been talking out loud. The door banged and in the mirror I saw Trevor appear from behind me.

"I saw your times for that rowing challenge they've got in the gym downstairs," he observed.

"I'm still a contender," I joked.

"Very impressive," he smiled, then he rushed out.

Tandy was still at my desk when I approached him. He saw me before I had a chance to say anything. He broke off from his dialogue with my male colleague. "How's it going, Ian?" he asked me.

"Well enough," I said evenly. "Got a ton of stuff to do, though," I added, and I glanced at each of them in turn.

"I was just leaving," he said. He placed his palms down deliberately against a clear space on the desk, then pushed up on to his feet. "And watch out for them flying coconuts!" he advised my male colleague as he shot out his cuffs. "Did you know your man was going to the Caribbean for the test matches this winter?" he asked me.

I did not reply. He turned and strode off down the corridor.

I typed in my password. Twenty new emails now sat in my inbox. Within less than a minute, my telephone rang. I saw Tandy's name come up on the display.

"Ian," he said. "Let's talk."

"I told you, I have a ton of stuff to get through."

"Fuck off you have. I'll meet you in the break-out area. Near the tea room in five."

I got there to find him already seated on the sofa. I took the armchair opposite.

"What was that about?" he wanted to know. Tandy never wore the same suit on consecutive days. More than once, it made me curious about his wardrobe space in the home he shared with his partner of the past three years. Today, he wore a white shirt, a black suit, a black tie with black patent leather shoes. If this contest was to be decided on sartorial criteria, then they could dispense with the interview and presentation now, and send me and Jake packing.

"I don't know what you're talking about," I told him.

"You're letting this competition thing get to you," he said, leaning back into the seat as if to get more perspective on my reaction.

I tried to remain impassive.

"And to no avail," he continued. "Because you know you won't get the post."

"I won't if the minute my back's turned you go about showing off to Kitson, by trying to ingratiate yourself with the team I've built!"

He twisted his neck this way and that around the room. "Where's Kitson?" he asked, shrugging his shoulders in an exaggerated fashion. He then straightened his tie, as if his recent movement had got it loose. "He's not even in today. You're not getting this job, Ian." His tone was triumphant. "You know why you won't get it?"

"Because, of course, you're going to get it?"

"Not quite. It's your walk. If you look at the people who get on in this place, what have they got in common? There's a senior exec walk. Now, you used to have it, but you lost it. You just don't walk like a senior exec any more, Ian."

"So are you're going to demonstrate your own walk while giving your presentation?" I asked him.

He scowled.

"Have you prepared it yet?"

"Have I fuck!" he replied.

I told him how calm he and Jake appeared, given that they faced losing their jobs in a matter of days.

He smiled mirthlessly. "If Jake's calm, it's because they've tipped him the nod. We'd be fools to think they haven't already earmarked their man. This presentation and interview – it's a kangaroo court!"

"Well, no one's come whispering to me."

"Me neither. But you're not listening, Ian. It won't be you. First, as I said, you don't have the walk, and second, being the youngest of us by some way, they figure you'll have an easier time moving on. It's all about Jake."

I'd watched Tandy at work over the years. While he spoke, I kept thinking that really he ought to be aware by now, that I was hip to his elaborate psychological games.

"Jake's taken out a new mortgage on a place in Stratford overlooking the Olympic village," he continued.

I said I didn't know that.

He worked his behind to the very edge of the sofa and dropped his voice in an effort to invoke a mood of confidentiality. "Now, Jake knew very well how Kitson was on this so-called restructuring project and the so called review that went before. Do you think a man like Jake would push an undertaking like a new mortgage if he knew there was even a whiff of uncertainty about his job?"

I shrugged.

"Don't think this is an open competition, Ian. They've already picked their man."

"So why are you so cool?"

"And don't be so possessive about your team, either," he continued, without answering my question. "These guys are running a book on which two, out of the three of us, are going to get kicked out of here."

At this point, my mask of implacability may have slipped a fraction. "How do you know that?" I asked him croakily.

"I was in the pub with Beresford from IT. These guys see all the email traffic they want."

I was silent as Tandy leaned back on the sofa, as if the better to observe his work made manifest by the expression on my face. "This is confidential, though," he added, and he was back on the edge of the sofa. He was like a prize fighter who, after ten rounds of hammering in the forearms and shoulders of his opponent, finally senses an opening. "So, no loyalty in this place," he pressed. His eyes were exultant.

"I guess not," I murmured. "Funny, though."

"That's why the two of us – fuck it, all three of us –

have to stick together, rather than get stroppy at the slightest thing."

"Please, I'm not getting stroppy."

On the Friday of that week, I shouldered open the gym changing-room doors on my way to a session on the rowing machine and walked in on Jake. It appeared he'd just finished his workout. He was fully clothed but for his trousers, his shoes and his socks. I saw his striped tie lying across his open sports bag. He was alone and standing before the mirror drying his hair. There was a moment of mutual embarrassment. Jake was the first to say something. He wanted to know how my presentation was going. I told him I had just started on it and asked about his progress. Like Tandy, he said he hadn't started on his. "That confident?" I suggested as I opened the closest locker to the door.

He turned off the dryer and sat himself on the bench running alongside the lockers. "I'm being realistic," he said. "It's not worth me putting that much effort into it. Don't get me wrong. I'm not going to disgrace myself in there. But it's clear that you and Tandy are the only real contenders."

"I thought you were the man, Jake."

"Think about it, Ian," he said, looking up at me. "What Kitson wants with the new product services director post is a man-manager. They don't need a technocrat. My skill set as a senior trading consultant just doesn't match neatly what they have in mind, with a large team and the coordination they'll need." He spoke like he'd been analysing this for a while. He started putting on his trousers.

"Besides," he said reflectively, "it's a young man's game. For the extra dough they're offering, there'll be more hours to squeeze from whomever they give this post to. I'm almost fifty now. They know it'll be harder for me to do than you guys."

Anxious to change the subject now, I congratulated him on the birth of his child.

"Thanks," he said. "When are you going to get started on your brood? You've been married a while now, right?"

"Ten years."

"Ten years married!"

"We got hitched straight out of university."

Jake was now fully dressed and he hoisted his bag over his shoulder. "Time to start knocking them out, youngster," he advised playfully. "But, on who's going to clinch this job – " he paused, and stared at me for effect " – my money's on you, Ian."

For her thirty-second birthday, I took her parents and mine for dinner at the Ivy. I came close to having to do some bended-knee begging to secure an extra seat because her parents brought along a tall, handsome guy whom it took me an embarrassing few seconds to recognise as Richard, her younger brother. Later that evening, I'd had an area of Just James's reserved for a few of her old school friends and our university pals to join us for cocktails and champagne.

I rode with her mother in the two-cab convoy to the cocktail bar. It had been a couple of months since I'd spoken to her. For the night, she'd worn a blue dress with a frothy tulle trim. Her coat remained across her bare forearm. A hint of glitter along with the freckles showed on her bare upper arms.

"You didn't mind me bringing Richard along, did you?" she leaned against my shoulder and asked, as the cab sped along the wet streets. My own mother was perched on the drop-down seat opposite.

"Of course not," I told her. Mother stared out of the cab window at the rain. She was no more than a few months older than Rita's mother and of similar dress size, but she would never have dared try an outfit like that. I knew and felt proud that, all the same, she would make no judgements. They were good friends. You could never go wrong with gatherings of our parents. I was more concerned about the mix of characters in the cocktail bar later.

"He's recently broken up with Jan," she continued. "And we didn't want him moping around his apartment this weekend."

I told her it really didn't matter.

Rita's cab got to the bar ahead of ours, and this suited me well. I wanted to observe her reaction when she walked in and copped sight of the old pals I'd had gathered there for her. I wasn't disappointed. Her shrieking reached us as soon as our taxi stopped and our feet hit the pavement outside.

Her father was less thrilled about the gathering. He would have liked more time with his daughter. From my corner spot, Rémy Martin in hand, I observed his busy frame circling the mass of burly shoulders and the coif-fured heads surrounding her – for ever outside orbit and looking very much the fan seeking to snatch some attention from a protected star. When eventually he resigned himself to defeat, I had a glass of Rémy waiting for him. He slumped into the space next to me, and the leather seat emitted a sigh just as loud as that coming from his mouth. He was not a happy man. Still, I discovered within minutes that he continued to credit me with more influence over his daughter's actions than I cared to admit I didn't have.

"Talk to her about it again?" he asked, turning sunken, watery eyes on me. He had a friend who still ran an English-language teaching school. He was convinced that he could find a post for his only daughter, if she showed some willingness and at least arranged for an appointment with him.

"She used to have so many interests as a teenager and all through university," he lamented. "It can't be good for anyone, not least someone young and intelligent, to remain home with no kids to look after, when she could be working."

I made some grunts that I hoped signalled acknowledgement rather than agreement with his views on this. One consequence of her chosen, employment-free lifestyle was her rigorous daily gym routines. Hour upon hour upon hour of gluteus maximus work, I surmised; for the fabric of her dress clung to her behind as if a football had been sliced and the halves, somehow still inflated, squashed alongside each other below her back. She looked lean, fit and ten years younger than any of the mates who surrounded her. And I was sure some had benefited from surgical touch-ups. I set down my drink and tented my hands to mask my hard-on from her dad. And in that pseudo-contemplative pose, and switching my gaze from his face to her behind, I listened to his lament. While he continued, I considered my own pitiful training regime. No morning sessions for fear of being drowsy during the day, and by the evening I was cutting corners on the leg curl and rowing machine in my efforts to catch the 7.15 and to get back home at a decent hour. Two more glasses of Rémy went down while I listened to her father talk of his employment plans for her. By now, she had moved to the bar and was in deep conversation with her brother.

It was at least a couple of hours before she approached to see what I was doing. She came forward, allowing her arms to fall limply at her sides, giving an exaggerated impression of exhaustion, but with a broad smile that said thank you better than any words could.

"Are you going to stay in the same spot all night?" she wanted to know.

"If I can," I said. "Good view from here."

By now, her father had glued his hip to his wife's in the face of moves by one guy whose attentiveness had begun to take an increasingly physical expression. Father was looking on, with an amused expression playing around his lips as he got filled in on the background to what was playing out.

Once she'd sat down beside me, it only took a few second for Rita to clock on, and she covered her mouth in mock astonishment and turned to me again. "Have you told them yet?" she asked. It took a second for me to fall in. "About what's happening in the office," she added.

I shook my head and kept staring straight ahead. "Hoping I might not need to," I told her. "I've got a few irons in the fire. Best thing will be if I can make a smooth transition without having to get anyone unnecessarily spooked."

Even before I'd finished the sentence, I glanced and saw that her face was already registering horror. She said nothing for a minute. Then, "You're ridiculous," she spat. She'd been sipping champagne for close on three hours by then. But still I was taken aback by her vehemence and how pained her expression looked.

"Why don't you tell them?" she demanded to know.

"As I said, I don't see any great need – especially on what's supposed to be a day of celebration. This one aspect of my life is spreading its tentacles into every little thing I do, it seems. I want to stop it here for once. Here on your birthday. It's your day, Rita."

"Bullshit."

"Did you say anything to my dad in the cab?"

She regarded me with horror. "No!" she said. "It's for you to do." She took a deep breath and surveyed the revellers across from us, before turning narrowed eyes to me. "You're fucking unbelievable, you are, Ian."

I was aware that, from a distance, the picture the others were getting was of man and spouse snatching a quiet moment to exchange confidences. In my head I was screaming for someone to save me.

"You're unbelievable," she repeated. And with that she rose, strode away and was swallowed up by her crowd of friends.

* * *

She was much more reticent once we were back in the house. While she showered, I lay in bed and turned my phones on to "silent". Your previous advice to us about a nightdress and decorum had flown out of her head. She left the bathroom and entered our bedroom dressed in grey flannelette pyjama bottoms and a creased, loose-fitting black T-shirt, and with her head turbaned in a white hand towel. She must have assembled that outfit specially from the "Man Repellent" section of the store. She paused and regarded me to check whether it was OK to turn off the lights. I nodded and she let her hand slide across the switch, and within seconds I felt her adjusting herself in her position at the near edge of the bed. The minicab ride home had been a silent affair. The booze, the food and the rocking motion of the cab had stirred something in me. I had stolen a couple of glances at her fishnetted thighs. They were within touching distance. But they might have been in Bogotà for any chance I had of getting between them in the next couple of hours without threat or maybe even injury to myself.

Lying in that bed, I was mindful of your dictum about not closing the night with unresolved issues of the preceding day lingering on. So I placed a speculative hand on her hip and quickly followed that with a query about how she'd enjoyed the evening. She returned my hand to my side with methodical care. Then, about a minute later, she spoke.

"I think I know what it is with us," she announced. Her tone was measured and clear.

"How'd you mean?"

"You know."

I thought I knew where she was heading. But I wanted her to spell it out. And it took some verbal coaxing before her tongue loosened up again. She confessed that, contrary to what I might think, she still did have amorous yearnings. "Amorous yearnings" – her phrase. She said she sometimes fantasised. I coaxed details, and there in the darkness she spoke of a heart-rendingly, long-running, fantasy featuring an avant-garde painter who, in her mind, she would visit in his unfurnished, unheated loft in Shoreditch. He'd be working on stuff for his first exhibition and she would visit him three times a week. Each time she would bring him cooked food packed into Tupperware and the visit would end with them clawing at each other on the cold floorboards of his studio.

I laughed humourlessly. "That's nothing but a dressed-up clichéd fantasy of an older woman for young dick!" I scoffed. I was stung and sexually stirred at the same time.

"I didn't say he was a *young* painter," she retorted. "The point is he's someone who makes me feel needed. Someone who doesn't need alcohol to get aroused."

"Bollocks," I said. She really did need a job. She'd imbibed daytime television psychobabble to a dangerous degree.

"Like, what did you think happened at that apartment that afternoon?" she continued.

At this first reference to that afternoon at your friend's apartment, my heart lurched. I closed my eyes and waited for her to continue.

But she paused, as if recalling the incident for the first time since it took place. "I mean, I had my doubts all along," she went on in a musing tone, then she stopped.

"But when I walked into that room," she continued, "and saw you sitting there with your legs wide apart with that self-satisfied smile on your face." She paused. "Then the way you got up and began undressing me . . . *Well,* I thought to myself. *If you're so self-contained . . .*"

"Self-contained?"

She continued. "*If you're so self-contained, then why don't you just go ahead and fuck your own self? Go fuck yourself,* I thought to myself. *You certainly don't look like you need anyone else. So go fuck your own self! Go fuck yourself.*"

She said our poor sex life had little to do with over-familiarity with each other and our surroundings, as you seem to think. She said she didn't need a fancy marriage counsellor like you sending her to strange apartments to get it on. She said she'd had a long talk with her mum earlier that evening and that she and her dad had been fucking every day since he'd retired.

"You talk to your mother about these things?"

"You've just got a knack for diminishing people, Ian," she claimed.

I said I didn't agree.

"You have," she insisted. Then she said my confidence got in the way of intimacy. "How many of your friends turned up tonight?" she asked.

"It was *your* birthday," I reminded her.

"How many would come to yours? I couldn't begin to organise a surprise birthday party for you!"

"Guys are different."

"Bullshit. OK. My brothers go-kart just eight kilometres from here on a Tuesday. Why do you think they never stop by?"

"Bad manners?"

"Because you're always over-the-top."

"Disagree."

"Take Christmas a couple of years ago . . ."

"That far back, huh?"

"No, just an example. I invited you to my parents' for Christmas. You knew my mum hadn't seen Andre for three years. I told you the problems he's had with his drinking. And you choose that Christmas, when we're all gathered as a family for the first time in years, to present her with a gold Cartier watch. And you didn't even warn me you were getting that!"

"Why should I have?"

"Listen, Andre wasn't even working at the time! How do you think it made him feel to see what he'd bought look so worthless compared to what you did . . . Did you even stop to think?"

"Bollocks."

"And that day when you bought champagne when we all went to Movida – "

I'd heard enough. So I interrupted her. I asked her, "So where do we go from here, then?"

She did not reply. I suggested another sit-down-and-talk session, with you acting as an external observer and occasional interjector.

"Look, I know you've got your interview to concentrate on," she responded. "Once we know the result of that, we'll have to talk, just you and me."

The Monday before the deciding interviews, Kitson arranged for Jake, Tandy and me to discuss ideas in response to an urgent code modification proposal that had been submitted by one of our rivals. One of our analysts had attended the first modification meeting and she was to give us a presentation before Kitson opened the floor to us for ideas and suggestions.

When the perky young analyst had got to her penultimate slide, I shot a glance at Jake. He looked as disorientated as I planned he would be. Over the past six months, I'd watched him perfect a technique for this type of meeting. I called it the "shoulder stand". He would sit himself to the right of Kitson, knowing the managing director's habit of going around clockwise to get our reactions and analysis in the face of a problem. Week after week, I'd watch Jake wait for Tandy and me to voice our perceptions first. Then he'd employ a two-stage process. First, with a nod towards the collaborative spirit, he would agree with some of our conclusions. But then, with the benefit of extended thinking time and our own perceptions, he would proceed to pick holes in our conclusions, and to close with some recommendations of his own, always loosely based on our earlier points. Then Kitson would thank us all for our contributions, especially Jake's incisive perceptions, and then Kitson would end up doing what he'd perhaps had in mind all along.

It was a technique that showed Jake in a good light at our expense. But that day I'd entered the conference room ten minutes early and positioned myself in his habitual spot. He'd shot me a raised eyebrow as he came in. I wasn't the least bit apologetic. It was a case of needs must. I was underprepared for the meeting. I'd asked my analyst to email me a briefing by close of play the previous Friday.

He'd called my PA that morning to say he was sick and I hadn't been able to catch him on the mobile over the weekend.

Jake began his session and, taking a leaf out of his book, I opened my notepad to annotate some of his conclusions. It was odd, but my view of the impending competition between the three of us varied. Sometimes, like Jake and Tandy professed to believe, I would think the result was as fixed as an 1980s wrestling match. At other times, I would think they had but a mere preference and that the real reason for the extended period before the interviews was for them to observe us during that time, and that we were under scrutiny all the while, that every meeting, every email request, every utterance, was monitored to discern meaningful differentiators between us.

Kitson was shifting his gaze from Jake to each of us in turn as Jake spoke. I accept that he wasn't the architect of this horrible situation the three of us found ourselves in. But I sensed Kitson was enjoying the execution more than he should have been – telling us six weeks in advance so he could watch us fight it out for our livelihoods, with him the ringmaster and us nothing but expendable pit bull dogs. He couldn't have dreamed a better incentive to productivity. Or a better way to demonstrate his ruthlessness to the board by executing this trumped-up review. *Look, I can cut heads, too!* The guy was as ignorant as he was callous. There was no way humanly possible that one guy could do our three jobs alone.

I wanted to avoid Jake at the close of the meeting, so I remained in my seat till the others had risen. I was the last to leave. I glanced back as I was about to close the door behind me, and there, beneath the seat lately vacated by Tandy, I spotted a yellow object. I bent down to retrieve it quickly, but Tandy had already disappeared down the corridor. Back-to-back meetings, his PA confirmed to me. I examined the object more carefully. It was a memory stick. I popped it in my inside jacket pocket. I'd asked him in the canteen earlier whether he'd completed his presentation and he'd muttered something about energy efficiency and only investing effort into winnable contests. I was sure that if I opened the files on that memory stick, I'd find him up to draft 170 of his PowerPoint presentation.

"Are you going to bet on yourself, then?" she asked me. It was Thursday morning. I had the day off and we were awaiting a delivery from the supermarket. I'd walked in on her while she surfed the internet in the study room.

"That wouldn't be wise," I responded. "I might as well throw the dough into the Thames. I'd put a bet on Jake or Tandy, but I wouldn't know who to give the money to."

"Still don't know who's running the book?"

"I don't think I want to know."

Judging from the images passing on her monitor, she appeared to be reviving her interest in hat design. Or maybe she'd received a wedding invitation that she hadn't got around to letting me know about yet.

"Who do you think it will be?" she asked.

"I'll be the one going," I told her.

She carried on clacking on the keyboard. "Why?"

"I met Trevor in the staff toilets the other day."

"So? Is he the office tea-leaf reader?"

"No, but you're not far off. Trevor's the chief operating officer. He's the man who looks after team budgets and all things financial. He would have the inside track on anything relating to departures and arrivals of senior staff."

"So you quizzed him. Tactfully."

"He didn't have to say anything. I mean, I'd taken a piss and he'd come out of one of the cubicles. I was at the washbasin and we exchanged greetings, that's all. And then he was out of the door."

"And?"

"Well, I didn't think much of it at the time, but lately I'm thinking that if you envisaged having an ongoing working relationship with someone, you wouldn't want them to know, and you wouldn't risk them letting everyone else know, that you're the type who leaves the shitter without washing your hands. But that's exactly what Trevor did. He saw me, and then walked right out of the door without washing his hands. You would only take that risk if you thought that soon you'd never see that person again. And it didn't matter what they thought of you."

She considered for a moment. "I think you're losing your mind."

"You think so?"

"I reckon."

"Well, maybe this will restore more balance." I held it up to her.

"What the hell is that?" she asked, staring at the yellow object.

"It's a memory stick," I told her.

That little object had been burning a hole in my pocket

since I'd retrieved it from the floor a few days ago. "And if we just place it in here," I said, as I stretched my arm over her shoulder to gain the USB port, "we'll know what Tandy's chances are, and whether he's been given a helping hand."

I had it millimetres from the port when her hand blocked the entrance. A cold clamp. "Did you . . . ?" she began.

"No, nothing underhand. I didn't pinch it. He dropped it and then he wasn't around to return it to. And then I couldn't think of a way to return it to him without feeling embarrassed."

"So you haven't looked at it yet?"

"No. Why'd you think I've brought it here? I wouldn't open it in the office. You never know what IT can monitor, as I'm beginning to learn!"

She rose from her chair as if the computer had suddenly become contaminated. "Ian, if you put that thing anywhere near there, I'll never talk to you again. I'm not kidding."

She was in fact deadly serious. Her eyes were unblinking. Her bottom lip trembled histrionically. But she'd misinterpreted my motives. I wasn't losing it, as she'd joked earlier, but it would have taken balls of steel to have remained unaffected by all the uncertainty surrounding our three futures. I glanced at the computer and the port stared invitingly at me.

"I assure you right now that this isn't about gaining an advantage," I told her.

"No?"

"It's not. After all the bullshitting from these guys, I

just want to confirm something in my own mind about what's going on with all this. I'm not going to try to copy his presentation or to look at it so that I can top it."

"I don't care, Ian. If you open his files, that's it. I can't believe you're even thinking about it."

"Look, babe, I've done my stuff already. If you look in the drives, you'll find it saved under 'Pres'."

"If that USB stick goes anywhere near that computer . . . that's it, Ian."

It was a childishly dramatic statement for her to be making. But her expression was frighteningly resolute. Without taking my eyes off her, I counted to ten, then tossed the memory stick towards the wicker bin in the corner of the room. I heard it hit the bottom. She stared at my empty palm as if to ensure she wasn't being made the victim of some magic trick.

"Hmmpf," she said, and she returned to her seat.

On the morning of the presentations I woke up ten minutes before the alarm went off. I went through my pre-work bathroom routine with the air of a sleepwalker. This in itself was not unusual for me on work days. When I got back to the bedroom, she was sitting up on the bed. She grunted something about ironing a shirt and I said I was OK. She glanced at the clock resting on the bedside table, rubbed her eyes, moaned and swung her bare feet back on to the bed.

I opened my wardrobe and ran my eyes over the suits arrayed before me. I fingered three or four and felt a pang of shame. I'd caught myself trying to make a decision about which one to wear, about which one would cast me in a good light in the eyes of my judges for the day. The feeling of shame resolved into self-disgust when for the first time I seriously considered the possibility that Jake and Tandy were right – that the decision had already been made and that this "interview" was a puppet show to mitigate the risk of future tribunal actions by the two they'd already earmarked for the chop. And how in a matter of hours I'd be seen by Kitson and the others on that interview panel as taking their puppet presentation seriously. It struck me then that there could be nothing sadder than a puppet parading delusions of self-determination before his master. Of course, to a benign puppetmaster this type of behaviour on the part of a puppet can come across as cute. But I wasn't sure Kitson was benign. And cute was the last impression I wanted to give to those guys.

It was hardly an opportune moment to fall so heavily into this type of thinking. But it was in this state of mind that I closed the wardrobe, opened the chest of drawers and carried a pair of socks and pants into the living room with me. I put them on while allowing myself to be mildly distracted by items on the breakfast news. Before too long, though I got caught up by one report, about the transfer of an Italian defender from Fiorentina to Liverpool, so much so that I was taken aback by her sudden appearance in the doorway. She'd thrown her dressing gown over her shoulders. I watched her bemused expression as she took in my semi-clad figure on the couch. Her eyes then travelled up to the wall clock above my head.

"It's eight twenty," she informed me.

"I know."

"We could go to the races," she offered.

"You don't even like racing," I reminded her.

"But you do."

I looked down at my wristwatch. "First race doesn't start till about midday," I warned her.

She nodded. "Well, if we could drive me to Selfridges first, we've got a deal."

"A hat, right?"

"How'd you guess?"

"Easily."

"I'll get ready."

"You do that," I said.

And, things have been OK with us since then.

HORS D'OEUVRES

Looking back after a month, nothing matches my first day in London as a student. I've had better days since and I've had worse days. But if we agree to go on strength and variety of emotions, the first day tops them all. A conversation with Lily soon after I got there is as good a place as any to start.

"Just promise this one thing?" she began.

Now, whenever someone kicks off like that, I get nervous. There was an almost rhythmic feel to the click-clacking that came through to us from outside the open door of the bedroom. Inside, Lily was standing a few metres away when she asked her question. I sat on the edge of the windowsill with my feet propped up on a wooden chair. I was staring at the bed in front of me. Her sad eyes were fixed in the opposite direction. She was staring out of the window on to the forecourt below.

"And what's that?" I asked.

Slowly, she moved from her position next to the window and took a couple of steps forward so that she could look me in the eye. "I want you never to be too proud to ask for what you need," she told me. "Can you promise me that?"

I had the feeling she would remain in my face until she got the right answer. I counted six beats on the click-clacking outside and nodded yes. She stepped away. The room was small but her steps echoed with each fall of her heels against the shiny parquetry. When she got to the door, she turned to face me again. She seemed restless and agitated and it felt strange seeing her like that.

"That's important," she continued.

She lowered her head and carried on forward until she arrived at the foot of my bed. She kicked the nearside wheel gently, then suddenly she plonked herself down so that the impact of her bum on the mattress caused her feet to rise high into the air. She smiled sheepishly at me and folded her arms across her chest. Earlier that afternoon, she'd helped me carry my chest of drawers from the car into the room. For her efforts, a chalky white patch showed on the side of the jeans skirt she wore. She noticed that my eyes had touched on it and self-consciously she brushed down her skirt with the heel of her hand.

As soon as she touched down on my bed, I'd given a soundless scream at her to get up. With what I had in mind for that bed, it just felt weird to see her sitting there like that.

I looked up towards the open door. "How're you getting on out there?" I called to Jim. I might as well have been shouting for help. At that moment, all I wanted him to do was to collect his wife and for them to leave. He, on the other hand, had convinced himself that unless he got this bookcase up before he left London, it would for ever remain as strips of pine on my living room floor.

Lily remained seated on the bed with a wistful expression on her face. I hadn't asked her, but perhaps she felt she had to do this. Maybe years ago her own parents had driven her down to London, stacked her fridge, put up her bookcase and tried to make her feel comfortable on her first day away from home. In any case, it had become clear to me that neither of them was in a hurry to begin their drive back up to Sleaford. While, for me . . . I was keen to get into the West End for the magic hours.

I'd been coming down to London on weekends and on the odd day during school vacations for almost two years. The high would begin as soon as I stepped off the train at King's Cross. It would increase in intensity as I caught the tube to the centre of town. It was a liberating feeling, too. Sleaford can be a closed place. Not many new people come in and not that many seem to move out. As a fourteen-year-old I used to be shy and, though I've changed a lot, back in Sleaford I don't think anyone will allow me to be anyone else but that fourteen-year-old boy.

So coming to London was liberating for me. But it wasn't something I could do whenever I wanted to. For a start, it was expensive. Then, it took ages. Also, it was a major distraction from school. Funny that it had taken Jim to suggest how the best way to get out of Sleaford was to get a place in a university down in London.

But, like Lily, even he had some promises he wanted kept. He entered my bedroom, swishing my table tennis racket. "I want you to continue developing your game here," he told me. I promised him that I would sign on to the university table tennis team before I signed on to the students' union. It was an easy enough commitment to make and it seemed to please him.

I walked them down to the car. Given my earlier feelings towards them, I wasn't prepared for the way my body reacted as Jim's head dipped below the far side door. Lily smiled bravely from the passenger seat. Her window had been wound down and I leaned forward to plant a kiss on her wet cheek. My hands trembled against the door jamb. So, so, embarrassing, but my eyes suddenly welled up. They were finally on their way. When I tried to say goodbye, a toad hijacked my vocal cords. Now this type of leave-taking is something that happens every year about this time, to a million eighteen-year-olds. I knew this. But it did nothing to lessen the impact on me. Here would begin the longest period of absence from the people who brought me into the world eighteen years ago. A ritual dance, a piercing, or some kind of sacrificial fire seemed appropriate to mark this: something more than just the brushing of lips on cheeks, the passing of digits through the warm night air. But then life goes on. Here was one rite of passage completed. I was hoping to have a more pleasurable one behind me by the end of the month. At least by the end of the month!

Within half an hour, I was heading for the tube station. West Ham station is on one of those over-ground lines, so before I got on the train I sent Theo a text message. I hadn't seen him in many months. The reason being that the sacrifice I'd made to ensure I got to live in London was to get my head down in Sleaford and clinch the right

A level grades for university. "I'm back in town", my message to him read. Nothing more.

At first I hated Theo. I would often see him when I came to the West End. I'd always catch the tube to Charing Cross station. Then I would walk up towards Covent Garden and I'd buy an ice cream from a shop in the piazza. I would do this whether it was summer or winter. Then I would stroll up to Long Acre, taking in some of the street entertainers on the way. If it was a weekend, I would make my way to Leicester Square at about 8 p.m.

The ice cream, the London vibe, the street entertainers, that sense that life, after so many fits and starts, was finally lifting off were all great, but on a weekend they were but the warm-ups to the main event. This began at about 8 p.m. – start of the magic hours. It was from about this time that the girls would begin making their way into the bars in the Square. They would be looking to have a few drinks before going to the clubs nearby. Now, in Sleaford you could go three months and in that time you'd see about the same number of girls whose boots you'd want to knock. In the Square, within ten minutes you'd see fifty girls like that. It was a feast for the eyeballs, that's for sure.

I found that from about 8 p.m. most of the fine girls would head to Yates at the corner of the Square near Capital Radio. On my first weekend down there, I followed a group of four past Burger King and all the way to the entrance. I watched them breeze through, with my tongue to the ground and my eyeballs popping out.

When eventually I mustered the courage to cross the

threshold of that tantalising joint, I found my path blocked by a thick, long and powerful arm. No words. Just an arm, about the same girth as my thigh, that came down and across my chest.

"No single guys, boss."

"You what?"

"Only mixed groups."

How were you supposed to meet someone if you weren't allowed to go in alone? Theo would say the same to other solo guys who tried their luck at the door. But if you hung around long enough, you'd see him wave through random single guys after giving them the black-man handshake. For weeks I watched this go on. But one evening, I did pull him up on his favouritism. Everyone could see he was letting his black mates in. I told him straight out that it was unfair. And that, beyond that, it was discriminatory, and that he of all people should be careful about these things. He turned down the corners of this mouth, then he gave me his broad back. He offered no explanation. This I took as the height of arrogance. I would join the crowd of single guys, the rejected, who would stand by muttering curses at him and the other, Middle Eastern-looking guy dressed in black who backed him up.

But it wasn't all bad standing out there. The view was great. A procession of firm tits, tight butts, long legs, short legs, filed passed our crotches and held our interests till they got to the entrance, only to be succeeded by the next procession of yet firmer tits and tighter butts. Once I heard one of the rejected guys say he'd knocked the boots of a short redhead he'd met in the roped-off smoking area outside the front doors.

The first time I actually got talking to Theo was once when I came down during the week. It was winter. It wasn't so busy and Theo was on his own, standing outside wearing a heavy, military-type coat complete with epaulettes and top pockets. I lit up and was just standing around having a smoke. Two girls came in from the direction of the Odeon cinema. After he'd checked their IDs, he'd said something to them in a foreign language and, surprised at first, they'd responded to him in what I imagined was the same foreign tongue. Theo watched them walk in, and then he turned back and shook his head as if unable to believe what he'd witnessed the first time around. He caught my eye on the way back and I smiled. He smiled back.

I felt encouraged to speak to him. "What were you saying?" I asked.

"Showing my appreciations," he said, in a thick accent.

"But what language was that?"

"Russian," he told me.

"You speak Russian?" I asked.

"I was studying there three years," he let me know. He pointed to his coat. "It's where this is from. But that was ages ago," he added. "During the communist times."

It turned out he was older than he looked. He told me he was forty-one years old.

"But where are you from?" I asked him.

"Angola," he replied.

"So that's four languages," I calculated. "English, of course, Portuguese, Angolan and Russian?"

"Add Mandarin to that," he let me know. "My wife's Chinese. I lived there for two years as well."

"What'd you study in Russia?" I wanted to know.

"Chemistry."

He never once looked at me for longer than two seconds during this exchange. His head and his eyes moved here and there, to the inside of the bar, up towards the Odeon, towards All Bar One, and they just caught me on the way.

What's a multilingual chemist doing working the doors? I thought to myself. I told him I was hoping to go to the University of East London to do Philosophy, and I suppose, because it was a quiet night, in between him pausing to check IDs and stopping single guys getting past those glass doors he listened to me. Things got busier later on. The girls began filing through in numbers. He caught me off guard when he turned and waved his thumb in the direction of the doors. He must have thought I was a dimwit because for a moment I remained rooted to the spot. It took my mind a while to catch up with even the possibility that he would let me through like this.

"ID first," he snapped, when he sensed my hesitancy.

He frowned down on the card I shoved into his hand. He obviously had an issue with my being seventeen.

"Only for one hour," he warned, wagging a finger and opening his eyes wide for emphasis. "Then back to your philosophy books." Then, finally, "No booze!"

Backless tops, miniskirts, low-cut tops – you only had to take one step past the door to view them arrayed at the front bar: a farrago of fabric, colour, perfume and flesh. How many shades of brown, pink and beige could you cram into a single, heavenly spot? Past the bar, I watched gobsmacked as they trotted past arm in arm on their way to the mirrors in the bathroom downstairs. It was Ladies' Night and I was a starveling, who, after spending months with his nose pressed to the restaurant window, finally gets the go-ahead to grab a spot at the top table. On that first day I paused after a couple of steps in – just to better savour the immensity of the moment. From that first day to the moment I'd put my London trips on pause, the intensity of feeling never dropped off. Not like with my first beer in a pub or my first time in the driving seat of a car. I always felt the same excitement in walking into Yates. In fact, it got stronger each time, and progressively as I began seeing how I might make the move from mere observer to successful participant in this feast of the senses.

By being "in with" Theo, I got to know the other guys who would come down to Yates. Like the legendary Dr Knockboot. This guy was less than a couple of years older than me, half-Irish, half-Colombian, but he'd knocked the boots of almost fifty girls. There wasn't a day I came down when this guy wouldn't be around. I would tag along with him to try and get to know the scene. I'd love it when he pointed out the girls he'd already knocked. Casually, he would mention it, like it was nothing at all. After a couple of months he would use me as his wingman when he wanted to infiltrate a group of attractive girls huddled near the bar or in the smoking area. Once I got talking to him about how hard it is to knock something without a car or without much dough.

He just laughed. "How long's the dry patch?" he wanted to know.

"Two months," I told him with a sorrowful shaking of the head. It was quick thinking. I'd have been finished in London if I told him I hadn't ever knocked a girl's boots. Not ever.

"You must be roasting!" he exclaimed.

Truth is, I must be the unluckiest guy in the world when it comes to that. Up in Sleaford a year ago I'd been going out with the vicar's daughter for six months. In the back of Jim's car one winter Saturday I'd been on the verge. But it was her time of the month. We arranged to meet the following week but her grandma died midweek and she was in no mood to even talk about the stuff I wanted. The following week I took this chick to TGI Friday's in Peterborough. We'd taken two steps out of the restaurant when she'd begun chucking up like a human fountain. I guided her back to the restaurant toilet to clean up, but it had put me right off her. On a quiet midweek night when I told Theo of these mishaps, he broke up laughing. He bent over in two, clutching his stomach. He was alone on the door that night, and while he tried to recover his composure single guys were filing through like it was a public park.

I'd question Dr Knockboot about what he'd say to these girls when he was alone with them. But he was always vague. "Fancy a philosopher not knowing what to say!" or "Just run some game on her", he would say. What was that? "Run some game"? My guess was he wouldn't be ready to give coaching tips when he was still in the game. Truth was, I was less interested in what he said, and I wanted to hear what not to say. Because I'm the kind of guy who could get things going, but then I'd say something stupid that would ruin the mood. Perhaps I was better off asking Theo. Theo, with his wife and his kids and his level-headedness. But Theo never has time for a sustained conversation. Theo is always interrupted by something in his earpiece, someone trying to push through or someone with a query. Years spent working on the doors meant that now Theo could only speak in soundbites.

If coming down to London was a feast, it was a feast where I was only ever allowed to get to the hors d'oeuvres. That's because I would always have to leave at 11.30 p.m. to get the last train home. That would happen all the time. Things would look like they were about to start kicking off in the bar, then I'd look at my watch and find I had to be making tracks to the station. That wasn't the worst of it. Knockboot would call me the following afternoon. The conversations would go something like this:

"Hey, student boy! You wouldn't guess what happened five minutes after you left the bar."

I'd say I couldn't guess.

"You know that girl who blanked me when I first grabbed her up on the dance floor? The skinny one with the green tights?"

"Yeah . . ." I'd say, dragging the word out while trying to visualise who he might be talking about.

"Well . . ." he would continue, and then he'd go into the some story, that would set my knob aflame and my concentration would be wrecked for the rest of the school day. Looking back, it was mainly thanks to Knockboot that I called time on my London visits in the run-up to my A levels.

But here I was, back now and ready to make up for lost time. And this time I would be gorging myself through the main course and into dessert. I wasn't looking to get back home before 5 a.m. I'd put on a pair of jeans and a T-shirt and I took a beige summer jacket in case it got chilly on the way back. I was going to ride this train to Embankment, then walk up to Charing Cross and through Covent Garden. At Mansion House station, two guys in dinner suits got on to the train. I noticed wet patches on their shoulders. Rather than walk in the rain, it might be best to change for the Northern Line at Embankment and head straight on to Leicester Square.

At Embankment, I made a dash to the Northern Line platform for Leicester Square. I figured I must have just missed a train – the platform was sparse for that time on a Saturday. I slackened my pace as I moved down the platform. The destination board said five minutes till the next train. I thought about grabbing a seat on a vacant row about a hundred metres down the platform when someone seated on one of the near-side plastic seats reached out a hand and pinched my arse. I felt it unmistakably. Someone from the row of seats had actually pinched my arse!

I wheeled around and glanced down at a smiling girl. She wore a smart, black dress. Her face was deeply tanned and offset by large gold-hooped earrings. Between her legs she held one of those jumbo plastic Pepsi bottles. After I recovered from what she'd done, I was transfixed by her eyes most of all – a deep shade of brown. Seated next to her was an older girl, who wore black trousers and a white sleeveless top and carried a gold-coloured handbag.

Six months ago, I would have sped off like a frightened rabbit. But the platform wasn't that full. I stopped before them and smiled. I imagined how Knockboot would have handled this situation and concluded that he'd have played it with humour. In silence, the girl with the hooped earrings raised the Pepsi bottle to me. *What the hell*, I thought. My hands brushed hers as I pulled the bottle from her fingers and raised it slowly to my mouth. Her large eyes looked up expectantly as I took a swig. Within seconds I was coughing and spluttering – this to the great amusement of the hoop girl especially. It was almost pure whisky in that bottle! I'd drunk whisky before. Plenty of times. But it was the surprise of it that had got to me more than the fact that it was so strong. Must have been six parts whisky to one of Pepsi. The hoop girl was buckled over laughing so that only the top of her head was visible to me now. She was on the end of the row of seats and I handed the bottle back to the older one, wiping my mouth with the back of my other hand. Then I took the vacant seat next to the hoop girl's companion.

"So?" I said.

"I'm Emily," said the older girl, extending her hand and smiling. "And this" – in between giggles she had to pause a while to compose hoop girl – "is my friend Brigitta."

"Yes, the one who molested me!" I joked, glancing at her mock-reprovingly.

They ignored me for one moment as they spoke in high-pitched excited tones and in a language I figured might be Italian or Spanish.

"I'm Harry," I interrupted them.

"Pleased to meet you, Harry," laughed the older one. "My friend Brigitta speaks only little English."

Brigitta beamed back at me. Then they were off again

in fits of hysterics as their eyes turned to a woman who shuffled past us in a pencil skirt and yellow clogs. It took them a while to recover from that one. They were definitely in good spirits. It turned out the girls were Brazilian. We got on to the train together. By now I was taken by Brigitta, the hoop girl. Completely. I had almost passed out when the train arrived and she stood up and I got to observe her figure properly. Magic. She was about my age. The other one was older, something like about twenty-eight, I guessed. She sat between me and Brigitta on the train. I asked them what part of Brazil they were from and the older one said they were from the south. I'd done some stuff about the German diaspora at school and I managed to guess they'd have German surnames. I was right. While I spoke, the older one translated for Brigitta. Her nods let me know she was impressed by me knowing of their German origins. Then I mentioned a few cities. They were from the fourth one I mentioned. Discarding Harry Buffey and using my Knockboot persona, I felt comfortable talking to these girls and my flow became strong. They were friendly and very loud, and I think that kind of put me at ease anyway.

Though I'd never met them before, I had a feeling of near instant recognition with Brigitta. I got the feeling just seconds into our physical exchange with the bottle. I had a premonition then that she was the one for me. Short term or long term, I wasn't sure. But I felt sure of the connection. She leaned forward in silence and whispered something to her friend in Portuguese and then Emily asked me where I was going.

I told them I was meeting some friends in a bar in

Leicester Square and then I asked where they were heading. They were getting off at Warren Street. The longer I looked at Brigitta, the more I discovered that got me hooked. She cradled the back of her head with her long, slender fingers. I averted my eyes. It was crazy. An erotic ideal had corporealised before me on a tube platform. In all my life, I'd only ever seen girls like Brigitta fleetingly in the passenger seat of another guy's sports car or two-dimensionally on top-shelf magazines at the local newsagent.

My palms were sweaty and the throb in my throat was near unbearable when that train pulled into Leicester Square. I leaned forward, placing my palms against my knees, hardly believing I had to say a regretful goodbye and push off. The door opened. I turned to Brigitta, who shrugged and smiled mournfully. Emily turned to me. She placed her hand gently over mine and her face became serious for the first time.

"Why don't you come with us?" she asked.

I glanced at Brigitta. She wore a gently amused smile. I watched the doors close. "Why not?" I said.

It was about seven o'clock when we rode on to Warren Street. Emily told me that they were sharing an apartment in Bayswater, but that they'd previously been in Preston and had only been in the apartment for three days so far and desperately wanted somewhere else to stay. The landlord was a real weirdo. Already I began getting frustrated with this language problem. Already I began wanting more than smiles and hot glances from Brigitta. Emily might have read my mind.

"Her English is very bad," she said.

Brigitta nodded.

"You like her?" Emily grinned.

"Well . . ." I began.

The train stopped at Warren Street and Brigitta stumbled as we made our way to the door. Emily extended a shaky arm in an attempt to steady her friend and she dropped the plastic Pepsi bottle. I retrieved it from the carriage floor.

"Tell me what you want to say and I'll tell her," offered Emily, after we were set on the platform.

"I want you guys to come to this bar with me," I told her straight. "The one in the Square." I said it just like that and I watched a look of concern cross her face. I reflected how it must have sounded to her to have what was to them a stranger, offer to take them somewhere they didn't know.

"We can't go far," she confessed to me. "We have to do something at half past." She paused. "But maybe after?" Again she spoke to Brigitta in Portuguese and Brigitta smiled and nodded at me.

"Yeah," I said.

On the escalator, they slipped once again into talking Portuguese. I sensed I had to keep their attention. "What do you guys do?" I asked.

Brigitta smiled. Emily translated for her, then responded. "Normally entertainment."

"Like?"

"Like singing, a bit of dancing. But we haven't done any in England yet."

"My mate's got an Equity card," I told her. "And I've got another mate starting at RADA in September."

"That's really good," she said.

Outside, the streets were wet but it had stopped raining.

My heart lurched at every glimpse I stole of Brigitta. We all stood under the station canopy. A minute of indecision elapsed, during which they spoke in Portuguese and I put on my jacket. I then stole another glance at Brigitta and reminded myself to remain cool. I've got the kind of mind that so clearly sees the goal in sight that I get overexcited and mess up the basic steps that got me in position in the first place. It would happen to me in table tennis when I'd race to a ten-point lead, then with three or four points left to close the game I'd lose concentration and the opponent would catch up with me. *Put the victory speech out of your head*, my coach would say, *until you're actually in the winner's circle*.

"Do you know where the Rafter is from here?" Emily asked. She was standing between me and Brigitta. Brigitta snatched the Pepsi bottle, raised it to her reddened lips and took another gulp.

I looked around to get my bearings. Everything was going for me. I'd been to the Rafter Hotel with Lily and Jim once before, when we stayed down in London prior to flying off to Venice. "I believe I do," I said. "Follow me."

"Let's go," she grinned, and we started off.

Brigitta skipped around us and linked her arm with mine so I was now between these two beauties as we strolled down Tottenham Court Road. The pubs were full, with couples spilling outside, beer glasses in hand. The red and white of the England flag draped store fronts and presaged the World Cup game later that week. In the offices above, wide-mouthed backroom staff pumped the air with their fists as managers announced they could leave half an hour early.

A fizz of expectation hung about the streets, a sense that at any moment the guy ahead of us, in yellow dungarees, would jump and click his high heels or the dad with the toddler further down would suddenly park the buggy and do a handstand on the kerb, and that everyone would laugh out loud but think it the most natural thing in the world. In breaks from studying, I'd had my dreams. After a hard day's revision, many a mini-movie had been produced and directed featuring the new Harry when he made his triumphant return to London town. If I'd dreamed the scenario I was walking through now, I would have left it lying on my mind's cutting room floor for being too far-fetched to be credible save to a madman.

There was a welling in my chest. But my breath came short, as if the air itself was infused with sugar and alcohol and I had to be careful not to take in too much. A giddy sensation took hold of me. I may have been borrowing Dr Knockboot's persona but the feelings were all mine. And, unlike Knockboot, one thing I wasn't going to do was just bang this girl and leave her. I was going to keep her as a friend. Both of them. Two polo-shirt-wearing guys glanced at us as they passed by in their van. Women on the pavement, too. *Who is this guy?* their faces said. The Pimp Daddy is who!

Emily asked if I smoked and I shook my head. Truth was, I'd given up since my eighteenth birthday. She broke off to get some Rizla and tobacco from the newsagent. Brigitta hesitated a moment, then shoved the Pepsi bottle into my hands with a smile and followed her into the shop. My phone beeped. A text message from Theo. I laughed to myself. The last time he'd seen me I was a green buck. I tried to imagine his face when I bowled into Yates as the Pimp Daddy with these two on my arm. I was hoping he wouldn't let on to Knockboot yet. Because watching that guy's face would be even funnier.

Emily was first out of the shop. She was grinning as she held a packet of Rizla aloft. Brigitta followed within seconds. They exchanged words in Portuguese. Taking in Brigitta's face and figure in that cocktail dress and heels for the hundredth time, I complimented myself for having persuaded Jim and Lily to get me that West Ham flat rather than have me stay in the student halls. Student halls. Even saying those words to girls like that would have been tough. Playfully, I imagined taking these two fine specimens of womanhood back there to its grubby communal kitchen, with little above cardboard walls to separate our night-time fun from the pricked-up ears of even grubbier freshers.

"How far is it?" Emily asked.

I pointed down the road. "Just there," I assured them.

She'd given Brigitta the task of rolling the cigarettes and I said how weird it was with her so sophisticated-looking in that smart dress yet rolling a cigarette like a tomboy. Emily laughed. But that was the thing about these girls. While most pretty girls I'd met had this aloof thing going on, these were the most natural, fun-loving girls you'd ever want to meet. Brigitta shot me a smile – one laden with unspoken promise. Emily told me that this wasn't her first time in London. Before going to Preston, she'd lived here for two months. But it was the first time for Brigitta. She told me Brigitta was nervous because it would be her first time working here.

"Are you working today?"

"She has interview," replied Emily.

"So you're here to give her moral support," I said.

She nodded. "How do you say?" she asked. "Moral support?"

"Yes," I said.

She seemed to like that phrase.

Still, once in the hotel lobby a silence fell between us. I figured Emily was the first applicant. No one else was around. Earlier they'd gone together to the bathroom and had spent quite a bit of time there. And Brigitta had emerged, gliding erect and even more ladylike than before. Now, we were all seated in separate floral lounge chairs, and with five minutes to go the only sounds were coming from Emily. I pulled out my mobile and texted Theo to get me and two others on the guest list for a really classy club. I told him I would be squiring two buff Brazilians to Yates and from there it would be on to the nightclub he suggested. Though Emily continued speaking in Portuguese, Brigitta had fallen into a worrying silence. I guessed she was concentrating on what she had to go through.

After a moment, a bearded guy dressed in beige chinos and a red T-shirt came to collect her. He wasn't smiling much, but he didn't look unfriendly. Though his hair was greying at the sides, he was very tall and his shoulders were rounded and broad under that red T-shirt. He reminded me of one of those ex-polo players. Introductions were made, and with a wave they departed for the lifts. Brigitta scooped Emily's handbag from the lounge chair as she trotted off behind him.

At the time, Emily didn't seem put out by this. But she soon became subdued. I assured her that English wasn't the guy's first language, so Brigitta need not get too stressed about her own failings on the language front.

"Where would you say he was from?" she asked me.

"Middle East or Spain," I said, without giving it much thought.

"Interesting," she said.

"What's the best movie you've seen in the cinema so far this year?" I asked her then.

She thought for a moment. "I don't think I've been to a movie this year," she reflected, as if surprised by that herself.

"Where do you live?" she suddenly asked me.

"In West Ham."

"How many do you share with?"

"Just me. My parents got me a flat. I start university in September, but I persuaded them to let me come down a bit earlier so I can look for work down here and start earning some."

"Did you find any work?"

"It's my first day," I let her know. "But I won't be rushing things."

She laughed. She liked that. "It's different for us," she commented, and her eyes wandered around the lobby. I sensed her discomfort.

"She's going to be alright," I assured her. "She looked in better shape than I would have. For my interview at UEL I got the sweats so bad about half an hour before time, you wouldn't believe! My dad had driven me down and he had to go off to the shop to get me a fresh shirt before I could go in there."

She laughed again. "What's UEL?" she asked.

"University of East London," I told her.

I hadn't *really* been nervous for the UEL interview. I only said it to make her feel better.

"Damn, she took the cigarettes with her," Emily wailed, raising her hand to flick back her hair.

I got the courage to ask why her head hair was dark but the hair on her arms was blonde.

"You ask a lot of questions, don't you?" she laughed, pretending to be annoyed.

I shrugged. But when I went on talk-strike, she soon came around. She sighed heavily and allowed her hairy blonde arms to fall limply at her sides.

"Do you like her?" she asked.

"Of course," I told her. "That why I'm taking you both out later."

She smiled. She spoke to me of Brigitta. Said she was a nice girl and deserved a nice guy. All the while, I prayed that Brigitta got the job. Girls can be moody. She'd been all smiles, but if she wasn't successful there was a chance she'd be in a foul mood for the rest of the night. I must have carried on speaking to Emily for half an hour. I told her my mate was a football agent and was looking to sign some players from Angola and might need some Portuguese speakers to help with translation. She didn't seem so keen on that idea and I began to have second thoughts about how much talking I was doing. I'd fallen for that one too often in the past: chatting to the ugly girl for such a long time that she starts thinking perhaps it's her I fancy when really it's the other one I want to get to. But there I caught myself using "ugly" and "Emily" in the same thought sequence. Emily was a fine girl. It's just that any girl would lose something next to Brigitta. Emily was ten years older than me, though. And they were friends. So I could only ever have one. And I preferred Brigitta. It was simple as that.

My phone beeped. It was a text message from Theo. He'd hooked up guest-list spots for Movida. But the longer I sat there waiting in that lobby, the more nervous I was becoming. Without her there, the euphoria of just twenty minutes ago had worn down to anxiety.

Emily stared straight ahead into the lobby. Now and again she would use just her thumb to beat a rhythm out against the side of her lounge chair. Every time our eyes met, she would give me a long, lazy smile without saying a word and on the next ping of the lift doors our necks would swivel in unison again to check if it was her.

More than an hour later, Brigitta caught us both by surprise when she arrived via the stairs rather than using the lift. She was alone. She sidled up to us. I couldn't read from her face if she'd been successful or not. She smiled weakly at Emily, who rose to give her a peck on the cheek. They immediately broke into Portuguese. It was understandable they would want to do that. I gave them their moment. But they went on for a long time. A hell of a long time, I thought.

There was a more businesslike tone to her voice now. I couldn't take it any longer. "Did she get it?" I asked Emily, when her eyes met mine for just a fraction of a second.

But she was far too engrossed in Brigitta's story to respond. They carried on their exchange for while. And then it became more heated. Eventually Brigitta tossed the handbag into the seat vacated by Emily and raised her hands to the back of her head and stood there staring blankly at Emily, then at the floor. I must admit dear Brigitta did look a bit ungainly like that. In any case, there was no eye contact for me.

"Did she get it?" I repeated.

The girls had another exchange and this time it ended with them hugging each other. Doggedly, I asked the question again while they were locked in their embrace. And this time, over Brigitta's shoulder, Emily winked in my direction. Relief! They remained in that embrace for a while. But for me, in that fraction of a second after Brigitta broke off, the weird thing was her glassy eyes: it was more like she'd lost something than gained anything new.

Emily retrieved the handbag and went to the bar to order coffees. I said I'd have a pint of bitter and slumped back into my armchair.

"Relieved?" I asked Brigitta.

"I don't understand well," she smiled. She remained standing.

"Do you feel better now?"

She nodded and smiled.

When Emily returned, Brigitta lowered herself into a seat. They sat sipping their coffees while I drank my beer, and they continued talking to each other in Portuguese. Emily broke off now and again to provide a translation. I reminded them that we should get going or we'd end up spending our Saturday night here in the hotel lobby.

Some repair work would have to be done on that bond between us before getting them to Theo and then into Yates and on to Movida. I'd never ever been to Movida before but I had the paper in my pocket, and at my side

I had two of the finest girls you could see anywhere. On the walk back to the station, I thought about snatching the middle position from Emily, but they were too involved in their conversation for me to crash in. I tried to catch Brigitta's eye, but she wasn't having any of it. I knew I had to be patient and to start things up again from scratch once we got to Yates. I'd be on my turf then.

At the entrance to the station, they stopped outside the ticket barriers and they began talking more animatedly in Portuguese again. Only rarely did they even glance my way. Every time they did so, however, I remembered to keep smiling. That's the advantage Knockboot had with being bilingual. Back at school, I'd have made more effort with languages if this link to my fortunes had been made. I was still holding the Pepsi bottle and I raised it playfully to Brigitta's face. She smiled tiredly. She took the bottle, thought about taking off the top, but then screwed her face up and waved it away. Mime was where we'd come to. She went on to examine the cracks in the pavement with the sole of her right shoe.

Emily turned to me. "Harry!" she called out in an upbeat tone.

I waited for her to continue.

"Thanks for helping us today," she breathed, and she was holding out her arms. I took a tentative step forward. I was unsure what was expected of me. "Look, you're such a sweet guy," she gushed. "But my friend so tired right now." She turned down the corners of her mouth. "Hug? I don't think we go out tonight."

I glanced at my watch once I'd come out of her embrace. "Well, it's only about nine thirty," I said hopefully. I managed to smile but my insides were collapsing. She might as well have put a wrecking ball to the side of my head.

"No, darling. I think we're going to take a cab." She extended her hand and a cab came screeching to the kerb.

I was momentarily dumbstruck. Panic crippled my legs.

The cabbie tooted. "Well, can I have your phone numbers?" I croaked. "Maybe going out some other time would be more convenient?" Even before I'd completed the suggestion, I felt the ball swinging again.

She opened her handbag. "Our phones isn't charged," she groaned.

Smash!

She took four short baby steps towards me. She turned down the corners of her mouth, then brought puckered lips to my cheek.

"It was great meeting you, Harry!"

"It was great meeting you guys."

Brigitta was already in the back seat. She waved from the window. I kept my eyes on the oval of that face for as long as I could as the cab pulled away and then disappeared down the road. I remained fixed to the spot on that wet kerb for some time. The Pepsi bottle remained three-quarters empty in my hand. I wasn't sure whether to continue to Yates or to simply return home to bed. When my phone beeped, I lacked the energy to even dip into my pocket and read the message. For a long while, what happened that evening was something I couldn't speak to anyone about. The huge sense of loss I felt was so disproportionate to the actual length of time I'd spent with her.

RUDY THE BANKER

I'd only turned the radio off because I thought I'd use the time to get some serious thinking done. But I'm the kind of guy who thinks best when he's in motion. And that Friday afternoon there wasn't much of that about on the Leytonstone High Road leading to Stratford town centre. The air conditioning was clapped out. I'd let the driver's window down and I might have been in Rome or in down-town Cairo for the honking and tooting and cursing ringing out in the hot and humid air.

I'd been stuck behind a red Mini Cooper for the past twenty minutes, during which time I'd progressed no more than a car's length. In my rear view mirror was a line of vans, cars and lorries that filled the rubber frame. When I hit the radio switch, I learned how a lorry carrying fertiliser had shed its load on the Romford Road. Police services were on the scene. They were warning home-ward-bound drivers to avoid the area if they could. I'd made arrangements for the shedding of my own load later that evening. The plan had been to get these groceries to mother and then head back across town to shower down and to meet the Australian banker guy whose number I'd taken at Reflex a couple of nights before.

I leaned forward in my seat. The leather had become a personalised inferno for my back. At the next left I exited the queue and pulled over. I parked up behind a rubbish skip at the side of the road. I wasn't going to roast in there along with the potatoes, carrots, poussins and duck in the supermarket carrier bag that nestled in the back seat.

Augustin didn't recognise me when I first walked in. At least, if he did recognise me, he pretended not to. The door had given a tinkle when I opened it, and he had glanced up but had quickly returned to sweeping the red rubber-tiled floor.

"Good afternoon!" I ventured.

"Good afternoon to you, sir."

He kept on sweeping. He wore a white, short-sleeved shirt, black trousers with pleats at the front that bulged at the pockets and narrowed at the ankles, with black, flat-heeled, slip-ons. He hummed to himself as he manoeuvred the broom this way and then that in the spaces between the empty burgundy leather seats ranged before the mirror that ran along the near side wall. As he progressed, he nimbly adjusted his feet in the manner of a dancer. He was humming all the while. To my eyes, the floor was already as clean as a corridor in a private hospital. I had the impression, based on not much at all, that he went through this motion for therapeutic rather than practical reasons.

What got to me with a force that surprised me with its power, was the scent of the place. There was a delayed reaction, but it went up my nostrils and into my brain, and for a few olfactory Proustian minutes it regressed my mind to days of short trousers and scalp-scorching embarrassments.

He carefully placed the broom in the corner of the studio next to an empty coat stand and then he turned to me with a smile. I realised in that moment that it had to be near on twenty years since I'd been there. I belatedly felt silly for expecting him to have recognised me.

I extended my hand to him. "Hi, I'm Ray. Miss Harvey's son."

He stared at me in silence for a moment. Then he looked me up and down. "Myrtle's son?"

I nodded.

"Me didn't even recognise boy! Jeeeesus, you have shoot up! You long man!" He sized me again up as if to make sure my story held. "It must be your father you take it from, because Myrtle no have height."

"Probably, probably."

"How is she?" he asked.

"She's fine. I'm on my way to see her now."

With an open palm he ushered me to the vacant seats.

"You're looking well, yourself," I told him. "You haven't changed a bit."

"Not that one," he said sharply before I could sit down on one of the leather chairs. I shifted along. "That's the one," he sniffed.

Considering the more or less sedentary nature of his work – he lived in the flat above, so didn't even have a walking commute – he'd retained the same slim build he had back in the days when my mother used to take me there on the first Saturday of every month. His hair, implausibly black as it was, still looked healthy and abundant.

"How long you here for?" he asked, rubbing scissors against comb with the deliberation of an actor checking his props before walking on to a stage.

"Just for an hour or two," I said. "Just to drop some stuff off for Mum. Have a chat."

"You come and go in one day?"

"Well, yeah."

He seemed slightly confused. "Where you living now?"

"I'm in Swiss Cottage," I told him.

"Your mother tell me you was in America."

"You must have misheard her. I'm in Swiss Cottage."

"But you were in America?"

"Never been there in my life."

"OK."

It came to me that I should have had a wipe-down before coming in. I feared that, with the heat and aggravation earlier, I might have worked up a funk. Too late in any case – he was already placing the bib over my shoulders.

"You want it shaved down?" he said, more in the way of a statement than a question.

I nodded.

"Skin?"

"Not skin. Leave some on there. Just a millimetre, mind. And please put a line at the back. And with pointed sideburns," I added as an afterthought.

He flexed at the knee, casting his eyes over my head as if to check out the terrain before embarking on a journey. I reflected on how many times he must have gone through that routine over the thirty-odd years he'd been here. How many heads must he have cut over those years? How many heads must he have observed mutate under his fingers from childhood heads, to adolescent heads, through to mature heads? Then he gave a little grunt as if he'd made up his mind how to press on. I noticed that, if his hairstyle had remained unchanged, the corrugations on his forehead and chin were so deep now as to create a pleating effect.

The maroon patterned wallpaper, the high ceilings, the row of chandeliers emitting yellowy light from above, the lightbulbs placed at intervals framing the mirror, the burgundy leather chairs – all conspired to give the place the feel of a rarely used theatre. Now all we needed was some music and a spotlight on us.

Years back, when I was a kid, more natural light had seemed to come in from the window that gave on to the main road. And when I started coming along on my own as a thirteen-year-old, the bass sound of dub music from the speakers would be constant, along with the risqué wisecracking from customers and the three other barbers working alongside him around those now empty seats. Some of the phrases and sayings I heard back then would only make sense to me years down the line.

He didn't say much at first, and that suited me fine. It might have been a generational thing, but there was not much I felt I could have spoken to him about. As a kid, when my turn came Mum would come up to the chair and they would both talk over my head, and with the bib over my arms I'd be powerless against the crossfire spittle that would coat my eyelids, nose and lips. I was hoping he wouldn't say anything sentimental about Dad passing away. After eight months, it still felt too raw to talk about.

To the solo accompaniment of his buzzing clipper, he approached his face to my cheek. A large part of the general scent of the studio came from his distinctive aftershave. I couldn't place the brand, but it had to be a line the manufacturers had kept running for twenty years. He started on the left side of my head and then moved on to the right. He moved to the left again, and when he got to my sideburns he moved in even closer. Surely a man of his age should be using glasses to do this. No? Maybe that was why he got so close.

The warm air from his nostrils rustled the fine hairs left on the side of my head, producing a tickly sensation. Good barber. He keeps his mouth closed on the close-up work. With some others their breath seeps from their mouths over your exposed head after having rolled over caked-up tongue and rotting molars. With those guys you need the lungs of a deep-sea diver. With those guys you curse every minute from their chair to your power shower.

The left sideburn done, he adjusted his feet to work on the line on the back of my head. His splayed fingertips pressed firmly against my occiput as he manipulated my head into position. Aaaah. Some shiatsu thrown in. Extra charge for that? I loosened my neck muscles to accommodate. I reflected. In London, barber studios remained the only spots where one black man could react voluntarily with such passivity to the delicate touch of another without fear of recrimination or injury.

I glanced at the mirror. A feeling of peace was washing over me. It so firmly replaced the angst that had possessed me earlier back in that car that the events might have been separated by years. I closed my eyes. Then, quite suddenly, Augustin excused himself and disappeared through the French curtains that led to the back of the shop.

I figured he'd gone for a cigarette. I took the opportunity to look around to check where the speakers were. I turned my neck this way and that. I couldn't find a source of music anywhere around. Five minutes quickly became ten. With my bib still on, I got up and stretched my legs. I stared outside and saw the traffic was easing up. My thoughts paused on the poor duck still stuck in the heat of the back seat of the car. I cursed myself for not having had the presence of mind to take the bags out with me. Then again, I was only half expecting Augustin to still be here, in East London, after all this time.

I returned to the seat and regarded myself in the mirror. I thought with an inward laugh that if I walked out like this, and simply left Augustin half the money with the job half done, and turned up on Mother's doorstep, she'd think I'd lost the other half of my mind. I glanced in the direction of the French curtains through which Augustin had disappeared. There were no footfalls, no sound of any movement taking place backstage there. I left my seat again and dipped through the French curtains into a tiny anteroom. Two of the walls were lined from floor to ceiling with brown unmarked cardboard boxes, which I presumed must have contained hair and cosmetic products. On the floor lay a face mask and a dusty teddy bear wearing a kilt. There was a black door. I tried the handle. It didn't move. I glanced at my watch and returned to the studio.

I hadn't recorded his departure time, but quite easily

half an hour must have elapsed. Half an hour! I was no longer able to remain in the chair. I paced the studio. I went back into the anteroom and placed my ear against the black door. All I got was a low whirr, like putting a seashell to your ear on the beach. I whistled a couple of bars of the Marseillaise. It was the first tune that came into my head. Nothing. I mouthed curses at him, his studio and my own stupidity for coming here in the first place.

Moments later, and quite suddenly, I heard movements back there. I remained on my feet but I had to consider quickly, exactly where to pitch my anger. The injunction not to antagonise those who prepare or serve food sprang to mind. Did this also apply to barbers? Fact was, he'd established that I was a one-off customer. So keeping me sweet and capturing repeat business wasn't an issue for him. If I was too strong, he might decide to do what the heck he wanted with my head. If physical appearance was a big deal to Rudy, then this errant barber could quite literally be holding the fate of the next twenty-four hours of my sex life, in his hands.

He reappeared with the clipper aloft in his right hand and shaking his head apologetically. I offered an expression of mystification rather than anger or even impatience. He glanced around the room.

"What happened to you?" I asked in a consciously even tone.

"Hey, don't tell me you chase all my customers away?" he glowered.

"I didn't do anything of the sort, man."

"You mean to tell me no one come in?"

"No one came through."

I watched the creases on his forehead deepen. "How'd you mean, no one came? This is Friday night!" He slammed the clipper down against the side countertop and panting, he stared out towards the window. He turned to me and raised his chin challengingly. "Just tell me what you say to them!"

"Look . . ." I began.

But then he suddenly broke into a grin. "I only fooling round wid you, boy." He reclaimed his clipper from the side countertop and motioned me back into the chair with a low, sinister chuckle.

"Is it going to pick up?" I asked after a moment.

He shook his head. "Things done changed here a long time ago."

"Can you do women's hair?" I enquired.

"Sure. Why?"

"Well, maybe you'd get more business from women if you advertised."

He paused. "You think your mother would come here instead of going to Ma Beechcroft, in Maryland?" He didn't wait for me to answer. "Of course not," he continued. "With hair, people go to their own. Women want women to do them hair."

"Well, perhaps you could manage female hairdressers?"

He did not respond. He was up to some close work on the back of my head now. When he reprised our conversation, his words made me think.

"Problem now is all the guys are going for shaven heads or for hair cut really low," he declared. He was now working on the top of my head. "That means them maintain it themself. And the technology make it easy for them now." He paused from his labours and held his clipper aloft for a moment. "See this? Before, you could only get one of these from a manufacturer or wholesaler. Now, you can buy it from the chemist."

My innocent question had set him off on a reflective train. "I started cutting in the seventies," he said. "That time big Afros was the style. And I was working in Mandeville, Jamaica."

"Must have been great days."

"Was alright, but guys would only come for trim. The best time was eighties, when Michael Jackson, Lionel Richie and Prince them had the Jheri curl look. Man! Every man them was running that look."

"That look was ridiculous."

"Me na care! That was the time I started as an owner here in London, young man. And it was the best time. Place was chock full of man, every single day. Man would be calling me on a Sunday offering triple price for a retouch. I had woman customer too, back then."

"I would never have had one of those."

"But then natural came back. But not Afro again, but fades or box cut. You know them would ask have the sides and back of them head shaved."

"Good times?"

"It was good. Got even better when them start wanting design and logo cut into them head like Nike or even leaf sometimes them want put at the back. But at the end of the day, anything that make things complicated and take more time was a good thing for me."

I felt momentarily guilty for not having asked for a

retro cut with my name cut into the side. But he was still on his tonsorial retrospective.

"Bad thing is this low-cut thing cross the board now," he continued. "All ages into those low cuts. Young guys and mature guys up to forty. The only group who want keep them hair on is older man like myself!"

"What are your competitors doing?"

"Me na worry about them, man. We all in the same boat. Some carry on with things on the side. If I wanted to sell trainers, I would have done that." He sucked his teeth. "But me na worry. Things gon change again."

"You reckon?"

"Ah yes. Everything changes every ten years. If that young boy with the slope cut do well in the hundred, the two hundred, the relays and the long jump . . ."

"What boy?"

"Julian Rawlings. If he do well in the Olympics, you'll see how his style will spread up. It take just one person individual enough to buck the trend and drop a different style in the public eye for everyone to turn and run it."

"What about Leo Blue?"

"Never heard of him."

"Singer with straightened, combed-back hair with a parting in the middle. Had a top ten record singing about beach life about a month ago."

"Oh, me know him. My granddaughter like him." He paused while he reflected. "But guys na gone run style of no batty-man," he said eventually.

"No?"

"Nah, man!"

"He's popular."

"With who, though? Nice, light-skin Jamaican boy leave the gal them and go have him shit press back by grown-ass man." He sighed. "You think him parents travel all the way to this country to have this happen to their boy?"

"Maybe he enjoys having his shit pressed back."

The buzzing of the clipper came to a sudden stop. I felt his eyes burning into the back of my head. "Them's not even things to be joking about," he said solemnly.

"My guess is only guys from the States dictate style to the world," I said moving things quickly along. "They're the trendsetters. It won't be an English-born guy."

"Not now," he snapped, switching the clipper on again. "You watch what me tell you bout the Rawlings boy in the Olympics."

"If he keeps his style till the final . . . If he reaches the final . . ."

"Him gone keep it!"

The door tinkled and in stumbled another customer. My heart sank. I prayed it was a first-timer and not a regular, because I'd had enough of Augustin talking now. I had to be on the road again. Things didn't begin promisingly. Though Augustin hadn't acknowledged the man's greeting, the newcomer had slumped into the vacant seat beside me with an alarming familiarity. From the corner of my eye, I could see he wore a baseball cap and carried a large, black, plastic bag.

"Can I help you, sir?" Augustin said after a moment.

"Maybe me can help you," the newcomer responded laughing. "Me have something for you here."

Augustin scoffed. "The best thing you can do for me is take you ass out of here. You na have work fe do?"

"I was on my way to the West End to do some business. But it look like me take me business elsewhere if this is what I'm hearing."

"What you have?"

"Yeah, you interested now!"

"Me na say . . ."

"Yeah yeah yeah, listen to him."

"Me na say me want anything. Me just want see what you have."

With a mock-withering look, the newcomer dipped down into his bag and Augustin paused but kept the clipper buzzing.

"What's that?" he asked, after the newcomer had taken out some items.

"Binoculars. Top quality, too. Once me reach the West End, all six will be gone in ten minutes."

"And what I'm going to do with that?"

"What you think? You have grandkids, ent you? Them study science. Them have birthdays and ting."

"Go away, man," said Augustin, and he resumed work on my head.

But for the buzzing of the clipper, there followed a long period of silence. No movements toward the exit.

"Hey, boss man!"

The change of tone gave me to think the newcomer was addressing me now.

"Hey, boss man!"

Augustin stepped in. "Hey, what I tell you about harassing my customers, already?"

"Say that again?" the newcomer demanded.

"You hear me well."

"Did I hear customers? Plural? I only see one person here, Augustin. But I have to congratulate you on getting someone in here at last. Long time I haven't see that!"

"You go on," sneered Augustin.

"Hey, boss man." The newcomer's tone was more insistent this time. "You interested in a bargain?"

I simply shook my head. To say anything would only have encouraged him.

There followed a longer period of silence, during which I heard the guy humming to himself.

"Hey, them Russian guys visit you again?" he eventually asked Augustin.

Augustin pretended not to hear.

"Hey, boss man," said the newcomer, touching me on the thigh. "You know two of them Russian guys offer to come take this place off him hand?" He giggled. "And him say he want keep it?"

I smiled. Only out of politeness.

The newcomer continued. "Them don't have black people round here no more. Why the hell you'd want to keep a place like this?"

"Them Lithuanian, not Russian," intoned Augustin impatiently. He'd completed the job and was reaching to the side countertop for the mirror to show me how it looked from the back.

"Whatever. They was making him a damn good offer for this place."

"How would you know what offer they made me?"

"But that's black people for you when it comes to seeing a business opportunity."

I rose from the chair to give the cut a closer inspection in the mirror running along the wall.

"You like it?" questioned the newcomer.

"I'm happy," I said.

"Well, that's good," the newcomer said. "Because you know he don't get much practice nowadays." He cackled and raised his hand up for a high five.

I shoved mine into my pockets. I wasn't going to get involved. I thanked Augustin and I pushed some notes into his extended hand before heading for the door.

"Give my love to your mother?" he asked and I assured him that I would.

When I glanced back, an odd feeling of sadness came over me. It was now almost seven o'clock. The newcomer was still seated. Augustin remained standing, broom in hand, and they were watching me as I waited to cross the road and get back to my car.

It was another couple of years before Augustin came back to mind. I'd walked into the living room just in time to catch Rudy flicking from one channel to another. I'd caught a glimpse of the image of a track in a stadium and thousands of spectators and I asked Rudy to flick back. He was seated on the rug with his back resting against the foot of the sofa with the remote control in his hands.

"It's sports," he sneered.

"I know that," I responded in the same pitch. "I just want to see one thing."

"You hate sports," he whined. But he got the channel back and he eyed me with mock-contempt as the camera focussed on the competitors behind the starting line. "You just want to ogle these fit young guys in Lycra, don't you? You can tell me."

"No, I'm not ogling."

"Come on, man. It's me. Since when do you watch sport?"

"This isn't just sport. It's the Olympic Games."

"Yeah, right. I believe you."

"Don't stress Rudy. This event takes no longer than ten seconds and comes only once in four years."

"A bit like you, then."

I ignored him. The camera panned across the faces of eight guys ranged before the starting line.

"It takes ten seconds but the build-up takes one hour," commented Rudy. He wasn't letting this go. "Do they really need to tell us where every one of those runners went to school and what their favourite dish is? Is it not just an excuse to keep the camera on them and to get those nut shots?" He sighed in exasperation. "This whole event is for the breeders and for guys like you who lack the nerve to get yourself some proper gay porn."

"It's the result I'm interested in, Rudy. And, as I said, it takes ten seconds."

"I bet you'd give anything for more than ten seconds with those," he teased.

"Stop already. You're like a fifteen-year-old today!"

"Well, I'm going for the guy with '459' on his shirt," he told me.

"I'm going for the guy with the sloping haircut – to win."

"That's just because he's a Brit!"
"Nothing to do with that, Rudy."
"Yeah, right."
"No, really. This is . . . this is something else."

THE APPRAISAL

There's no learner manual for the neophyte contract killer embarking on a career without secret service experience behind him or her. There's no formal qualification, complete with accreditation and badge, that you require before you can make that first sangfroid retreat following a close-range head or heart shot. As a profession, we'll for ever be dependent on the oral tradition. And that's why it was always worth me pinning my ears back when conversation with V strayed into the detail of his past work.

V operated all over the world. I was still on the force when, perhaps in desperation owing to scheduling issues, he'd passed me my first two jobs. If the need for education kept me listening, it wasn't only the pedagogical spirit that kept him talking. Support systems for people who make a living by ending the lives of other people are limited. Even the most trustworthy and open-minded person he could risk speaking to about these matters would rightly see his world of pills, silencers and phials as belonging to a sordid cartoon. In any case, his was a solitary existence. Like me nowadays, he spent much of his spare time with his head between the covers of books.

He could only ever realistically speak to selected fellow practitioners about work-related stuff. I thought I saw the transactional arrangement here. I was in need of tutoring, and he could sometimes use a non-judgemental ear.

We sat on a row of plastic seats in Charles de Gaulle airport. He was en route to Boston when he spoke to me of his retirement from "civilian" work. By his account, the trigger event was a job he'd gone to do in Chelsea shortly before Christmas last year.

I would never dare ask V who he got his jobs from. I accepted all work he would pass me without question about stuff like that. He would only ever subcontract English work. I still reckon most of his work falls in the sociopolitical category: a few years ago, a couple of US rappers poisoning the youth with their audio-crack and more recently a terror-friendly ogre posing as a politician in Asia. These were passed to him by contacts from his secret service days, but his paymasters would sometimes use him if they needed domestic stuff done – a bit like bunging a few quid the way of the phone company guy to put in that one extra line.

The Chelsea job was supposed to have been a straightforward execution that he might have passed to me if he'd had anything better to take care of. A freshly divorced chinless wonder was affronted at having to cede the former marital home and to pay alimony to a former partner. This was all supposed to look like a burglary gone disastrously wrong owing to the "have-a-go-heroine" attitude of the intended victim. In total, he'd clocked up about five hours of recce and prep work before he turned up at the house. He got there at 9.00 p.m. and set himself in the loft. He was expecting a confirmation call at 11.15 that night to confirm that he'd completed on that job.

His recce work told him the target would be home alone by 10.00 p.m. When it got to 10.10 with no sign of the imminent departures of her guests from that living room, his mind ran to contingency measures. At 10.15 he eased his forty-five-year-old, world-weary frame down from the loft. At 10.20, dressed in black, with white gloves on and carrying a small white canvas bag in one hand and a Ruger with a silencer in the other, he stepped into the living room and considered for a moment that his work might already have been done for him. The intended target lay writhing on the floor, trussed up and gagged.

In the room with her were two people, a young woman and a young man whose collective ages didn't amount to his own. The young woman he identified as someone who came to the house twice a week to do the cleaning and other domestic chores. The guy, perhaps on hearing his footfalls from outside the door, had prepared himself and was wielding a long screwdriver. He was about six foot tall, with cropped brown hair and wearing a ripped blue T-shirt and jeans.

"Now," V said as he moved further into the room, "how all this ends up is completely down to you. So, keep your voices as low as mine at all times and let's take it step by step." He stared down the young man. In modern-day London, he was counting on a guy that age to recognise a real Ruger when he saw one. "Step one. Can I ask you both to rest your palms flat against that far wall? Can I ask you, young man, to put that screwdriver down first?"

He waited for the two youngsters to move to their

positions, arms stretched out and palms flat against the wall. He sidestepped towards the woman who lay on the floor. He examined the bindings around her hands. He tightened her gag, fixing it more securely around her mouth and leaving her nose free. Then he looked up again to make sure their eyes hadn't wandered. He checked the young man's jacket and the young woman's coat; he took out their mobile phones, turned them off and placed them into his bag. "Just stay where you are," he warned when he caught an involuntary movement from the young guy. He looked a shifty one.

V stepped up to them, and with his free hand he began to rummage through their pockets. He shovelled out coins, Travelcards and pens and he placed them on the low coffee table. Then he held up the young woman's student ID card.

"Sabrina Copley," he read out loud. "Student. But then again I know a bit about you, don't I? I've been your neighbour here as you've gone about your work for the last few weeks."

She was still too disorientated to talk. He turned to the guy. "How about you, young man? Apart from the bit I overheard earlier, what I know about you is from hearsay. Can't find any ID. Are you secret service? Terrorist? James Bond's protégé?"

"Neither."

"Right, young man. Start talking to me, then. But don't move. Remain right where you are. Both of you. Give me your address, date of birth, current employment status."

"Right, I'm Cyrus Arrowsmith. I'm living rough at the moment. I'm eighteen years old. I've left school. I'm just an average guy."

"Before you started living rough, where did you live?" V asked. "And remain with your eyes to the wall."

"At my parents' house."

V stepped towards the trussed-up woman again. "Where, boy? Where do your parents live?"

"Wapping. Franklin House, London."

"Kick you out, did they? How many of you lived there and up until how long ago?" While he spoke, he held the prone woman's head in his hands. There followed a terrible cracking sound, quickly succeeded by a muffled groan that caused the youngsters to instinctively turn their heads in its direction.

"Look straight ahead!" V warned them. "And keep talking."

"My mum, my brother and me," Cyrus continued falteringly. "I was born there. I'm a local lad. Everyone around there knows me. I get along with everyone around there."

V remained silent for a moment. "Could it be because you're such a gentle, sensitive guy? Do you think that's why?"

"Please," responded Cyrus. "If you're undercover then I have to tell you that this is a domestic. I didn't mean no violence. Nothing was taken. You can ask her. We all know each other here. I've known this girl here since we were kids, basically. This is her boss, Lindsay. We were having an argument, that's all."

"You haven't been listening, and that might just cost you in the end. I have a real issue with the definition of domestic bliss you're painting. The fact of the matter is, I've walked in here to find your girlfriend falsely imprisoned and an air of fear in the room and the owner of the house stone cold dead on the floor!"

The two youngsters wheeled around. Lindsay's gag now lay around her neck. They watched her upturned face in horror. Her eyes were still open, her mouth agape. Sabrina screamed.

"Hey. This has gone too far, man!" shouted Cyrus.

Sabrina rushed towards Lindsay's sad figure, but V intercepted her and stopped her movement by grabbing her narrow wrist.

"She's dead," V informed them.

"I want to go now!" Sabrina shouted. "Get me out of here right now!"

"This has gone too far!" protested Cyrus.

At this point, V felt that he had to re-establish some order. "You're both raising your voices above the acceptable level," he warned them. "If it's because you're nervous, I might let you off - for a moment. If it's because you think we've already established some level of familiarity, then you couldn't be more wrong. Now back up, both of you. Move to the wall!"

I had looked up to V as a master of the craft. I didn't interrupt his story, but at that moment I thought I'd identified his error. He ought to have taken Cyrus and Sabrina out even before completing on Lindsay. But then again, if he'd taken that course, the planned "burglary-gone-wrong" scenario might have had more difficulty holding up. I listened on.

Sabrina began to sob uncontrollably. She was a dark-skinned black girl with large brown eyes, average height and with a cane-row hairstyle. Up close, she had much more vibrancy than he'd imagined she would from the long-distance photos he'd taken during the recce.

"Unless you're especially altruistic," he told Sabrina, "I wouldn't worry too much about her." He pointed his gun in Lindsay's direction. "Her problems are all behind her now."

Sabrina turned red, tearful eyes upon him. "Just let me go, please. I want to go. I want to go. I want to go."

"Now, Sabrina, stop this," demanded V. "You want to stop this and turn back to the wall. Because I'm going to fucking lose patience and execute both of you little runts in a second!"

Cyrus made to curl a protective arm around her. She shrugged him off.

V continued. "We've all got a more pressing concern here. Lindsay's left us. She's gone. She's never coming back. And what I'm saying is that, at this moment, you ain't got the luxury of grief. I, and as a result you, have an immediate issue to resolve."

He fell silent for a while. Perhaps he knew then that his hesitancy had put him in a bind. He opted for candour. Perhaps it was the easiest way. "Listen up," he said. "We have a problem here. And we need to solve it. Because your very lives depends on it. I'll explain. My people are going to call me at 11.15 p.m. Got to answer two questions before I can reap the fruits of my long labours. The first question they'll ask me is – job done? And second question – all clear? Now, for question number one, I'm OK. I intend to answer fine and dandy. As you can see, she's not breathing." He paused. "But how can I answer number two without lying? See, they will ask me if everything's under control – with no possibility of any comebacks. Now I can't say yes with any confidence with you guys still around, can I?"

Cyrus spoke first. He coughed and cleared his throat. "Look," he said. "All we want to do is get out of here, like nothing's happened." He tilted his head in Lindsay's direction. "This is the first time I've ever met this woman."

"Look, I'm no risk. I don't know your name or anything about you," added Sabrina.

"For your good health, we'll keep it like that – for now," replied V.

Sabrina raised her hands to her cheeks. "I mean . . . Believe me, all I want to do is walk away from this."

"No, I believe you," said V. "I understand how that would suit you. But you still haven't grasped the position here. I've worked with these people for a good long while now. They're a nervous lot. And understandably so. It's a high-risk business we're in. And in close to half an hour they'll be checking too. I'll be honest with you guys, because in the circumstances I think you deserve it. The only reason you're still breathing is because I'm slightly thrown." He turned his back to them for a moment and took a couple of paces forward. "I've never waxed anyone under thirty in my civilian life before," he said reflectively.

"Please, Mr . . . Just let us go," Sabrina pleaded, perhaps taking instant heart from his confessed indecision.

"But you've got to be more creative than that," he added. "That's why you ain't got time to be distracted by Lindsay." He strode over to Lindsey, lifted her and placed her on the sofa. "You've got to get creative. Because, when that call comes, I intend to answer both questions with confidence."

"Have you got children of your own?" asked Cyrus. "You know, little ones?"

"Hold up," V interrupted. "Don't get me wrong here. A little tip before you eat more into your time. Eight years, I've been in this game. Never mind what I told you, emotive stuff will have as much impact on me as no impact on me. You'd best simply think of a logical scenario that will allow you to leave here. That's enough to be getting on with."

A cowed Cyrus remained silent.

V glanced at his watch. "You've got to get over your fear and start thinking. In this game, I've observed how too many people fear death. What I . . ." He pointed his gun at his chest for an instant. "What I fear more than death . . . Do you know what I fear more than death?"

Cyrus shrugged.

"Incarceration. Society is a prison enough – imprisonment of the spirit. Physical incarceration on top of that is more than I could ever bear. I'd take death over incarceration any time, if they were offered me as options. So, if you want me to let you walk away from this . . . no more clumsy emotional pleas. Because basically, you'd be asking me to risk my life for yours. Now you have the picture." He paused. "But I'm a compassionate man. I'll give you both twenty minutes to convince me I should take a chance and risk my life for yours. Right now, I'm too tired to be creative. Told you I'm not that creative by nature. Appreciate creativity though. Perhaps now more than I used to. Convince me why I should risk my life and let you live. You've got twenty minutes."

Cyrus kicked off first. "Look," he said, "I can tell you now that not a word of what we've seen will ever, ever, leave this room!"

"How can I be sure of that unless I wax you both?"

"Cause I swear we won't repeat what we've seen. We've seen nothing. That's the truth. We never saw him do anything, did we?" asked Cyrus, turning to Sabrina.

"I didn't see anything," confirmed Sabrina.

Cyrus took a deep breath and turned his body to regard Lindsay's figure on the sofa. "If I had to swear on the Bible saying that you did anything to her, I wouldn't be able to do it. Because I didn't see anything. I wouldn't do it!"

V fought to repress his exasperation. "What's that worth to me?" he asked. "What's the incentive on you to keep your word? Well, I know where you both live. And let's face it, if I let you go right now, the fear still fresh in your bones might stop you singing tomorrow. But what happens after one year, two years? What happens then? Sooner or later I'm going to get that knock on my door."

"We won't. I promise!" cried Sabrina.

"Talk to me properly, girl – not like a dur-brain – or I'll have to plug you in quicker time than I'd even intended. I was expecting more from you, especially. You're the first person who'll be pulled in if I let you walk. You'd be the last person to have seen Lindsay alive!"

"But no one knows I work here! Absolutely no one. Well, apart from you – and . . ."

Cyrus cut her off. "Fact is, we won't breathe a word to police. And parents. I'm not even talking to my parents."

V considered them in silence for a moment. "OK, let me have a go with an alternative scenario," he suggested. "Maybe it'll spur your creative juices. Here goes. Enraged and homeless youngster, kicked out by parents, with a penchant for violence, he bursts into the house of his longtime girlfriend's employer. There, he discovers what he'd suspected for weeks – that the trollop's seduced his girl into a lesbian relationship. In his rage, he kills Lindsay Tait. On sight of the dead body, his girlfriend becomes hysterical. He panics and in his red mist he kills her in an as-yet-to-be-determined way. He then flees the scene of the crime. The search will continue across the country for his whereabouts. What'd you think of that?"

"Please Mr . . ." began Sabrina.

"Oh, I figured you wouldn't be loving that one," observed V, sneaking another glance at his watch.

"Listen," said Cyrus. He adjusted his feet and placed his palms more firmly against the wall. "What about . . . what about what's between us?" He shifted his feet again and pointed at his chest, then at Sabrina, before placing his palms back against the wall. "Me and . . ."

"Eh?"

"Have you ever been in love?" he added.

V laughed derisively. "What'd you say, man?" He stepped up to the youngster.

"I asked, have you ever been in love?"

"Are you just hard of hearing or thick? Haven't you heard what I've been saying? Have you been listening to me? You do pick your moments – to take the piss. Your cost, though!"

Cyrus stifles a sob.

"Sorry, but am I being too hard here? Have I just taken a turn into another zone in time and space? Or are you not the same guy who with a shandy down him was about to ram his knob up a woman old enough to be his mum the moment he thought his girl was twenty-five metres away? You little ho. Now, seconds later, I'm expected to take a chance on you and risk spending the rest of my days in a rotten jail because you say you're in love?"

"Please, just let me go," wailed Sabrina. She'd stepped away from the wall and had turned her tear-stained face to him.

"I swear, I mean what I said," continued Cyrus and he too turned to face V.

"I should let you both go because you love each other?" V asked in an incredulous tone. Ruger still in hand, he turned away from them, paused, then turned to face them again. "Love," he said. "Love – it fizzes, sizzles and then it fades. Tell me, kids. What has been the payoff for love to our society and culture?"

Cyrus and Sabrina exchanged a look registering utter mystification.

"A handful of dodgy poems, pop songs and narratives?" he suggested.

I couldn't help thinking then that these were neither the words nor the actions expected of a man who'd spent this long in the business. As he spoke, I could not help but count in how many ways I would have played this differently.

"That's not true," protested Cyrus.

"You'll be missing nothing, I tell you that," scoffed V. He stared more conspicuously at his watch. "You guys aren't doing very well," he commented, as he stole a glance at Lindsay. "But concentration was always going to be a factor in this kind of situation. Maybe you're thinking ahead about your own personal pain. Trust me. It'll be no worse than a visit to the dentist. Don't mind this gun. It's only here to deter you from doing something crazy. It never is my instrument of choice. I think anyone you kill deserves a personal touch. I try, circumstances permitting, of course, to do that."

"Personal touch," Sabrina sneered. "Thanks. Well, that's makes me feel so much better. Makes me want to straight jump for joy! Can I ask you as a human being to stop this?" Suddenly her tone had become challenging.

"I'll hate to do this as much as I expect you'll hate to see it done," said V evenly.

"I don't deserve this."

"How can you do this?" chimed Cyrus.

V stepped over to the pharaonic head. "I noticed you developed an attachment to this," he observed. "She'd offered it to you, hadn't she?"

"I asked for it a few times," replied Sabrina.

"Do you know I used to fancy myself as an Egyptologist when I was eleven or twelve. Liked everything about it – that kind of . . . vibe. The feeling of being in communion with the ancients or with some lost and forgotten wisdom that I might be able to get even a slight hold of . . . just by being there, perhaps. Egypt. And I got to go there as well – as an adult. I did."

"I'd like to go," Sabrina told him. "Did you like it?" Her tone was hopeful. Her large brown eyes scoured his face.

"What a fucking let-down. Yeah, a fucking shambles. All these fantastic structures. To gaze upon, to enter into, to contemplate. Structures that took the efforts of thousands over scores of years to erect. And all for what?

That's what stuck in my throat when I got there – but only when I was actually there in front of them . . . You've got to actually be there to feel it. All for what? Just because a bunch of rich, idle fuckers were too cowardly to face down death like every other man, plant and animal. Had to have their dead bodies mummified and hidden down there in those catacombs with all the treasures they thought they could take with them." He paused as if to recollect more fully that disappointment. "What a fucking miserable attempt to extend their selfish and frankly fucking useless existence. But the actual primitive stupidity of it all only hits you when you're out there in front of those monstrous fucking monuments to ignorance and vanity. But by then it's too late, see. You've already paid your airfare, wasted hours of your life. And to add insult to injury, you've got the locals trying to flog you camel rides round the fucking gaff. But I'm digressing. And that's not good for you, is it? You're giving me an accusatory look, Cyrus."

"I'm not. I mean, I wasn't . . . I was just looking into space."

"Probably thinking what a fucking hypocrite you are," said Sabrina.

V laughed incredulously. "What was that?"

"You heard," she repeated breathing heavily. "I said he was probably thinking what a fucking hypocrite you are."

"Yeah?"

"That's right."

Cyrus stepped in. "She's tripping, man. Sabrina, look . . ."

"Let her run with it," insisted V. "I want her to say her

piece. Just think, if you had a friend of yours lying dead on a sofa. Say your piece, girl."

"Sabrina, wait," said Cyrus.

"You injure and you take the lives of innocent people. You're a thug. Who takes lives."

"Is that it?" sighed V. "Don't expect me to be ashamed of that. Millions live. But are they living a life? I don't think I've ever taken a worthwhile life."

"You say."

"Are you actually living a human life? Is it possible in the world we're alive in?" Centuries from now people will look back with horror on the barbarity of our times. Don't be fooled by the suits and outward facade of sophistication. Empty vessels. No more spiritually evolved than the fruit flies. At least I never made the mistake of taking technology for sophistication."

"You're a murderer," she pressed.

"I prefer 'recycler' myself. Or maybe 'evolutionary agent'. Just doing my best now to create an environment better suited for real human life. Later on, maybe . . ."

"Don't patronise me because you've got a gun, Snoopy! Don't patronise me because you've got to rely on force . . . on violence . . ."

"Force and violence," he repeated. He pronounced the words like he'd heard them for the first time.

"You use threat and violence when most people have left those ways to the animals!"

He glanced at his watch again. "What people, though? Your naivety's cute. But cute ain't going to cut in the position we're in."

"Can I say something?" asked Cyrus.

He ignored Cyrus. "You see, most intelligent people only abandon violence as a tool after they've secured their interests."

"Can I say something?" insisted Cyrus.

"Go ahead," V relented. "It's in your interest."

"I know you said you had no kids. But look. We're youngsters, man. You can't be doing this to us. We've got our whole lives ahead of us. The things you're saying. Well . . ." Cyrus made a motion with his raised hand to indicate that it was way over their young heads.

"Yes, I did admit I was thrown by your youth. Outside of the army I haven't killed anyone under thirty. And that was ten years ago now. So, I should let you go and risk my incarceration simply because you're young."

"That's not what I said."

"I'm supposed to risk my life for yours because you're young? Across this world kids younger and more gifted and more deserving than you two die by the minute – through starvation and lack of drinking water." He snorted and turned his gaze to Sabrina. "Youth and youth culture," he continued. "So dominant, but so poor when you look at it. When I think on what Western youth have contributed to the world, I can't say I'm that impressed. In fact, I'm hardly impressed at all. What's it good for? Courage in battle, sport, music, fucking, poetry. Poetry, well . . . maybe a certain type of poetry, lyric poetry. Not good for much stuff beyond that, really. Lyric poets die young. Creatively, they know they're not much good for anything else beyond a certain time."

The youngsters regarded him quizzically, perhaps

convinced now that they were in the presence of someone who was deranged in a way they hadn't encountered before in life or in fiction.

Cyrus's voice emerged choked and distorted. "Look, man. Not sure what you're on about but everyone was young once, man. Even those who eventually grew into the people you respect and admire now."

He shook his head. "People I respect and admire," he repeated. "But even these people. And they number very few – alive. They're . . . they're . . ." He broke off. "It's a sick, sick, sick world, Cyrus. A world guaranteed to stunt the spiritual growth of all but the superhumanly strong. In a lifetime, what I've found almost without fail is that anyone under thirty who isn't a revolutionary or who hasn't committed suicide in disgust at the world is one of three things. ONE a corrupted fucker, TWO just born evil or THREE stupid. Now, which one are you?"

He'd lost his veneer of cool and had raised his voice when he asked the question. Cyrus's face was panic-stricken. "Man, if it's spirituality you're talking about," he began, "I don't go to church. I can't stand here and tell you I'm a regular attender. But . . ."

V interrupted him "By mentioning religion and spirituality in the same breath, you've just now placed yourself in the category of the stupid. Now, where are you guys going? What do you want to do? You're both, what . . . Nineteen? Twenty? You've probably already clocked up a million hours of television between you. You're probably cankered beyond hope. In spiritual terms, you're probably both terminally ill!"

"You don't know enough about us," pleaded Cyrus.

"You're saying I'm wrong?" he asked, returning to calm mode.

"You don't know enough about us."

"Now you've had your say," V then told them. "Shall I tell you what I think of you both – so far? I reckon the least I can do is be frank with you – given the situation we find ourselves in. Do you want me to tell you the impression you two have given me so far?"

Cyrus nodded almost imperceptibly.

"From what I've heard, I just don't think you're as disgusted at life as decent or intelligent people should be. You're much too happy. Which leads me to believe that you're either already corrupted or irredeemably stupid. Now, the question I need to answer is this. Should I risk doing a lifetime of bird for anyone falling into those categories?"

"I'm at university," Sabrina reminded him.

He waved her down. "Right! And are you connected with any organisation dedicated to the reform of this mess that we call our civilised world? Tell me what groups you belong to."

Their faces registered confusion. "How'd you mean?" asked Cyrus.

"Any environmental groups?"

"No."

"Women's groups?"

"No."

He regarded Sabrina. "OK. What about black organisations?"

"No."

"No? But, sorry. I apologise. How old-fashioned of me.

No need any more, is there? Why would you? Because it's all good, right? Is that how you guys say it nowadays? It's all good." He turned his attention to Cyrus. "What are you doing now, son? Are you connected with any organisation dedicated to the reform of this mess that we call our civilised world? Tell me who you're connected to. And if you lie to me – because I'm going to check your wallet for membership of even basic groups like the Red Cross – I'll blow noodles out of your brain right now!"

Cyrus's mouth shaped to utter some words. They never emerged.

"You're not a member of any such group?" pressed V.

"No."

"Do you play sport?

"Not so much now."

"Nothing. Yeah. I knew it. You're just a couple of cunts, really. Sorry, am I being premature? You're going to tell me I've got you wrong. Anything from the case for the defence? I tell you what. Maybe I should open things up. Be a little bit more objective. People talk about psychological profiles and that, but I tell you what . . ." He stepped sharply back over to Sabrina's leather tote bag and Cyrus's wallet. "In the absence of other stuff, there's a lot about a person can be discovered by a more detailed look at the contents of their wallets and stuff. The seeds of their tomorrows could be all there to be discovered." He roughly prised open Sabrina's tote bag and dipped his fingers inside. "OK. A folded-up newspaper . . ." He gave her a searching look.

"Found it on the tube," she told him.

He returned it to the bag, paused and then regarded

her again for a few seconds. "I thought you travelled by bus."

"I was late and took the tube this time."

He continued his search and pulled out lipstick, a hair clip, lip balm, banknotes and mascara without comment. He then pulled out a leaflet.

"Buddhism," he said musingly. "Who gave you that?"

"A woman in Stepney."

"Did you take it out of guilt, curiosity or interest?"

"Mixture of all."

"You didn't even remember you had it, did you?"

He delved into the bag again. He was pulling out stuff and dropping items on to the floor.

"Mirror, tokens, receipts. What have we got here? Supermarket receipts. Hey, lottery tickets. Play every week?"

"More or less."

"Those carrots. They keep us hoping, don't they?"

He continued his foraging. "OK, what have we got here? A memento. A photograph!" He paused and regarded Cyrus. "I've got to break it to you gently, young Cyrus. It's not one of you. Not unless you used to have tits."

"That's Sue Smith," explained Sabrina.

"Right. How long have you known her?"

"Met her in the first year of uni. She's my best mate."

"She know you work here?"

"No."

V dropped the tote bag to the floor and retrieved Cyrus's wallet. "Blockbuster Video card. How often do you take out a movie, Cyrus?"

"About once or twice a month. Used to."

"What's the last DVD you borrowed?

"An old one. *Notting Hill 2*."

"And what was that about?"

"It's an old one. Was about this guy and this woman from America . . ."

"Stop there. OK. You got some Rizla. Library card. You visit the library often?"

"Often enough."

"Right. Now, what have we got here? Hmm. Hashish." V held the wallet high and allowed the rest of its contents to fall to the floor. "Seems you like your altered states, man."

"What do you mean?

"Hashish, films, books." He paused. "Not like reality much?"

"Well . . ."

"Tough for you?"

"Not specially."

"Well, well."

"I do write music. I've got a CD."

"Oh, your stuff. Heard some of it. Any good, you reckon?"

"I think it is."

"Let's hear some more. Let's hear if it can save your life. Let's hear if it's worth risking my life for." V removed the disc from the table and made for the CD player. He placed the disc into the portable CD player and waited for the first tune. He skipped through the tracks. "Where'd you get this done?"

"In a studio. In Wardour Street."

"How much time it cost you to get this done?"

"Been doing it off and on for about a year."

"About a year?"

"Just about, yeah."

V remained standing as he took in the rhythms coming from the speakers. It wasn't a good thing for V to listen to that music for any length of time. After a moment, he glared at the CD player, detached the flex and then ripped it from the socket. The whole thing brought out the worst in him and he set to smacking Cyrus over shoulder and head with the flex.

"Children starving on three continents and you spend that amount of time locked in a room to come up with a piece of shit like this! With all the time and resources at your disposal, as a young adult in one of the richest lands in the history of this planet, this is all you can come up with in a year?" he panted. He dropped the flex and without catching his breath he marched to the canvas bag and retrieved Cyrus's mobile phone. The younger man watched him intently as his gloved fingers moved over the keyboard. By the time he'd finished, his breathing had returned to normal. He turned the phone off again and placed it back in the bag. With a glance at his captives, he ripped a sheet of paper from a notepad in Sabrina's bag and scribbled some words. Then he tore the paper in half and summoned Cyrus to the arm of the sofa.

"Please," breathed Cyrus.

"Silence, man!" V pointed him to the strips of paper. "Copy the words I've written on to this blank page," he ordered.

Cyrus advanced with trepidation. He fought every impulse to glance at Lindsay's motionless body. On one of the strips was written, in an almost childlike hand, five words. "Sorry. I can't go on."

"Please, man!" screamed Cyrus.

V raised the Ruger. "Just write it, Cyrus!" he barked. "And sign underneath when you're finished." V examined the results. He squinted at it with suspicion. Then he skipped over to Lindsay and rolled her off the sofa. "Your probation's over, kids. You haven't entertained me and, alas, I haven't found anything worthwhile about you really. You've come up with nothing. So, now I'll have to waste you both!"

"You can't do this!" screamed Cyrus.

"To the wall again!"

There was a ring at the front door. The three regarded one another in silence. The bell sounded again. V raised the Ruger to head-shot level and pressed a finger to his lips. There was a shuffling of feet outside and then silence. There followed a cough, then more shuffling of feet and, moments later, the sound of a car pulling away.

"Where was I?" V asked.

"You can't do this! Tell him why he can't do this, Sabrina!"

"I think she's already told me and showed me all I need to know."

"Talk to the man!" screamed Cyrus.

"Something you need to tell me?"

Sabrina was silently sobbing.

"It won't just be us you're killing," stuttered Cyrus. He was taking short breaths and his face was bright red.

"No?"

"No."

"Well, you'd better explain."

"It'll be four people you'll have killed."

V glanced at Lindsay's prone figure. "Four people," he repeated. "Look, are you playing with me, boy? Do you really think you've got the time for this? Cryptic's not going to cut it for you here. You'd better start talking straight."

"She's pregnant. There's four of us here. Five of us. Four."

V's face was picture of scepticism. "Who's pregnant?"

"Tell him, Sabrina."

"She is?" V questioned. He turned to Cyrus. "I understand the desperation," he remarked.

Cyrus raised his hands imploringly to his face. "It's why I've been kicked out my home! It's why we've been saving up. It's why we're both working all the hours God sends, because, whatever happens, we'll need the extra. That's the truth!"

V stared challengingly at Sabrina. "Whatever happens," he repeated. "Whatever happens. What'd you mean by that? What does that mean? 'Whatever happens.' I mean, she's either going to have a kid or she's not. What's this 'whatever happens'?"

After a moment's silence, a knowing smile spread across V's face. "You mean you're both debating whether to have it or not?"

"I do. We want it," Cyrus said.

"So, she doesn't want to go ahead," V suggested. "She wants to get rid of it?"

"No, that's wrong," corrected Cyrus.

"She was working to get rid of it."

V took her chin between his gloved thumb and index finger. "How far gone?"

She said nothing.

"How far gone?"

"Three months," said Cyrus.

"Three months. Fancy that. I've got to take a moment here. Sorry. Really, I beg your pardon, but I've got to take this in."

Ruger still in hand, V lowered his other hand and placed it over her stomach. "How far has your doubt taken you? Some reading? Few telephone enquiries? Trip to that doctor? Fancy that. After all this, we find that we have something in common."

"Fuck off," she spat defiantly.

"Do you feel morally superior to me because you've got a doctor as an intermediary?"

Cyrus stepped in. "You've got it wrong, because she hasn't made up her mind to do anything of the kind."

V glanced at his watch. Only a few minutes remained before the expected call asking whether he'd completed. At this point in his story, V turned to me and asked how I would have closed on a job like that.

Reckless candour might not have been the best course. I had to consider this carefully. Half of me wanted to tell him I wouldn't have allowed things to get that advanced; half of me was coming to suspect that the point of the story was less about therapy for him and more about testing my suitability for future work. The recession was swelling the range of types willing to take on domestic work. Clinging doggedly to the entrepreneurial spirit and beguiled by the promise of zero taxes, self-autonomy and the low level of bureaucracy in the sector, these guys were flooding the market and hurting the pockets of existing practitioners. The low competency thresholds were another factor. To a guy with a healthy appetite for risk you couldn't dream up a market with lower barriers to entry. Have hammer, will work. And so they kept coming. You only had to hear the crime reports for five minutes to learn of their clumsy antics that left trails that led not only to their doors but to the golden portals of their paymasters, to know that the game would soon be up. Somehow some kind of standards had to be introduced. These were the guys striking terror into the hearts of those even toying with the notion of granting a go-getter a contract on a former spouse, a boss or a competitor in sport or business.

V continued. "Given what I'd seen of those two, what was the probability I'd be putting the lights out on one of us? And their kid. Given what I'd seen of them, a child no sooner born than stifled by the fumes of the corrupt society and a world they were both doing their best to perpetuate . . ."

He was off again and I cut him short. Because it had suddenly come back to me. I took a deep breath. "It was a difficult one," I told him. "But what I think all of us guys need, just for us, is some kind of social club."